Stories for a

Dead Night
In
Spokane

Stories for a

Dead Night
In
Spokane

Dark City Books

All the characters and events portrayed
in this work are fictitious.

Death at Sunrise, *The Serious Business of Ira
Hammerstein*, and *Foolproof* copyright 2009 by Colin
Conway.

A Good Girl is Hard to Find, *The Skating Party*, *Death
by Radio*, *An Act of Mercy*, and *Under Angel's Wings*
copyright 2009 by Barbara Curtis.

Indecision copyright 2009 by Robert Beaumier.

Payback copyright 2009 by Dan Webster.

Firebug copyright 2009 by Dale Alling.

Work Ethic, *The Vacation*, and *Hired Help* copyright
2009 by Steve Oliver.

Dark City Books Edition Published July, 2009
(email: darkcitybooks@darkcitybooks.com)

Stories for a

Dead Night
In
Spokane

The Serious Business of Ira Hammerstein
By Colin Conway

On July 17, Ira Hammerstein woke several
minutes before six a.m. He lay in the darkness of
the bedroom, listening to his wife, Rachael,
snoring softly next to him.

After awhile, Ira reached over and turned off the
alarm clock that was set to sound promptly at six.
He sat up, swung his legs off the bed, and slipped
his feet into a pair of leather slippers. He stood up,
straightened out his pajama top and repositioned
the bottoms. Once adjusted, Ira shuffled quietly
from the bedroom into the kitchen.

He started a pot of coffee brewing before
retrieving the newspaper from the front porch. Ira
returned to the kitchen, sat at the table and began
reading the paper, as he did every morning. His
eyes scanned several stories before he sighed and
shook his head. The news of the day no longer
held any relevance for him. He carefully folded the
paper and placed it at the front door for Rachael to
take with her to work.

He wandered into the reading room, just off the stairway, and selected a collection of Mark Twain short stories. Ira returned to the kitchen, poured a cup of coffee and sat down to read his favorite short story: *The Notorious Jumping Frog of Calaveras County.*

Shortly after seven a.m., Rachael walked into the kitchen. She was wearing a brown pantsuit with a large broach over her left breast. Her short, brown hair was perfectly coiffed, and her make-up was, as always, neatly applied. At forty-two, Rachael was still the most beautiful woman Ira had ever seen.

Rachael poured herself a cup of coffee before turning to her husband. "Already done with the paper?"

Ira nodded. He had finished reading his favorite Twain tale and was now absently flipping through the remainder of the book, looking for familiar passages that might make him smile.

"Not going in to the office today?" she asked.

"No, I think I'm going to call in sick. Take a mental health day, so to speak."

Rachael studied Ira. He hadn't missed a day of work in five years. The last absence was due to passing a kidney stone. Ira loved his work as auditing supervisor for one of the largest accounting firms in Spokane. "Do you feel alright?" she asked.

"Sure," he said and sipped from his cup.

"Okay," she said, with a little shrug.

Rachael walked over to Ira and leaned in to kiss him good-bye, her lips stopping a millimeter before touching the skin of his forehead. She made a smooching sound and stepped back.

"Have a good day," she said and left the kitchen. Her perfume hung in the air for several minutes after the front door closed.

When Ira finished his coffee, he put the cup in the dishwasher and returned the short story collection to the reading room.

Ira detoured to the bathroom and took a leisurely shower. He dressed in a pair of black slacks, black loafers and a white polo shirt.

Once he was dressed, Ira entered his study and removed four large envelopes from the bottom drawer of his desk. Three of them had been sealed and addressed the day before. The fourth envelope, while full and sealed, was not addressed.

Ira took the three addressed envelopes and left the house. He mailed them at the nearest post office with return receipts requested. He was careful to keep his proof of mailings, as well as the receipt for the charges.

When he returned home, Ira gathered up the unaddressed envelope, a pad of paper, a roll of Scotch tape and a pen. He sat down at the kitchen table and wrote a three-page letter.

When the letter was complete, Ira returned the notepad, tape and pen to his office. From the closet, he pulled out the Colt M1911 that his grandfather had carried in the Korean War. Ira had cleaned the pistol several times each year following trips to the gun range.

Ira pondered the religious implications of what he was about to do. He was born Jewish, but had converted to Christianity twenty years ago to woo and marry Rachael. Both faiths were now distant memories to him, but he was sure his soul would be condemned, if it had not been already.

Ira walked into the bathroom, climbed into the bathtub and closed the shower curtain. He put the gun to his temple, asked his oft-forgotten God for forgiveness, and pulled the trigger.

When Rachael returned home from work shortly after six that evening, she immediately sensed something was wrong. There was a strange smell she couldn't place, and a feeling of dread pressed in on her.

On the kitchen table was an oversized envelope and a folded letter. Written on both items were the words "Read before calling emergency services."

Rachael froze as these words sank in. She backed away from the table, turned, and hurriedly searched the house.

She found Ira in the bathtub. At the discovery she screamed. She sobbed as she rushed back to the kitchen to call 911.

She lifted the telephone receiver and heard the dial tone. Then she saw the envelope and letter again and her finger hovered over the number pad. She put the receiver back and returned to the kitchen table.

Rachael opened the letter and began reading.

My dearest Rachael,

I have always loved you and must admit I still love you. You were my first love and have remained my only love.

My only wish is that I could have been that for you.

Rachael stopped and reread the last sentence.

> *My only wish is that I could have been that for you.*

Her mouth went dry. She pulled out a chair and sat at the table.

> *I know about you and Henry Ralston. I discovered your infidelity by accident, as I had always trusted you. I found a repeated number on your cell phone bill that you were calling late each night after I had long gone to bed. It only took a little ingenuity and the Internet to discover who that phone number belonged to.*
>
> *I am sorry to confess this, but I hired a private investigator to follow you around the past two months. I had to know for sure because my suspicions were eating away at me.*

Rachael lifted her hand and covered her mouth.

> *The pictures that were taken of you and Henry were not flattering and were damaging to me in ways you would not understand.*
>
> *Even with the pain and embarrassment you caused me, I couldn't confront you. You always chided me for not fighting for the things I wanted at my job, but you always allowed me to back down*

from you in our relationship. Maybe that is why you started seeing Henry. Perhaps it was my being twelve years your senior. Or maybe it was something else.

Regardless, I wanted to confront you, but I didn't have the courage. I couldn't stand the idea of accusing you of this and truly losing you forever to Henry.

Instead of facing you directly, I talked with Ronald about my discovery.

Rachael whispered "Oh, no" through her hand. Ronald was Ira's oldest and dearest friend. He was also the owner of West Land's Construction Company, and Rachael's boss. She was employed as the company's bookkeeper.

It did not surprise him to learn of your infidelity. He suspected as much, but was hesitant to bring it to my attention. Upon my revelation to him, he asked me to audit all of his accounts. He had begun to suspect money was missing, and he believed you to be responsible. He hadn't mentioned it before because of our friendship, but did admit he was close to challenging you about his suspicions.

After some considerable research, I found what you were trying desperately to hide from both Ronald and me. I didn't reveal my findings

> *to Ronald because I wanted to find where you had hidden the money.*
>
> *With the help of the private investigator, I finally found your account at the credit union. The $20,000 is still there. I did not attempt to remove it.*
>
> *You may or may not have found my body by now. I could not have faced you with all of this, so I took what some may consider the easy way out.*

Bile rose in Rachael's throat and she ran to the sink to vomit. She shook for several minutes as she struggled to regain her composure. Once she felt strong enough to continue reading the letter, Rachael returned to the table.

> *In the envelope are copies of your cell phone bills, your credit union account statement, the photographs of your infidelity and the general ledger showing how you stole money from our friend. I've included a detailed summary on how I found all of this information and how it proves your guilt.*

Rachael tore open the envelope, and its contents spilled out. She shuffled items around until she knew that Ira was indeed telling the awful truth.

> *I have sent a copy all of these materials to Ronald, the police*

department and the newspaper. The first two are obvious in their intent. The packet to the newspaper is to guarantee the story gets out. Your father's friendships won't be any protection from the police department as long as the newspaper is watching.

Taped to the last page of this letter are the post office receipt and the proof of mailings to confirm this to you.

You can call the police now and report my death. I am sure, however, that they will have more questions for you tomorrow.

I finish this letter, Rachael, by saying that I still love you but can never forgive you for what you've done.

Ira

Rachael cried as she looked at the evidence Ira had accumulated against her. She knew her life was ruined unless she figured a way out before calling the police to report Ira's death. She picked up the phone and called Henry. She told him about the letter, the evidence and how copies of everything had been sent to the police and the newspaper.

"You're on you own," Henry said.

"What?" Rachael said, not believing what she'd just heard.

"I didn't steal that money. You did."

"But you encouraged me to do it."

There was a pause before Henry said slowly, "That will be tough to prove in court."

"You bastard!" Rachael said, "I need your help."

"Like I said, you're on your own."

With that, the phone went silent.

Rachael cried for another hour as she tried to think of a way out. In the end, she went to the bathroom and retrieved a short bottle from the medicine cabinet.

She looked at the body of her husband in the bathtub. "Why, Ira?" she asked. "Why?"

She returned to the kitchen and filled a glass with water. It took a while to swallow all the pills in the bottle.

Rachael lay on the living room couch and cried herself to sleep.

On July 18, an envelope arrived at the West Land's Construction Company. Another was delivered to the police department. A third arrived at the newspaper office. None had a return address. No one was identified as the envelope's recipient.

The mail clerk at each location opened the envelopes to discover whom to direct the correspondence.

Each discovered the same thing inside the envelopes.

Thirty pages of blank paper.

A Good Girl is Hard to Find
By Barbara Curtis

Spokane, 1968

Vickie Lynn Hargrove gazed out the window as the bus rattled south across the Howard Street Bridge. She noted that as the mornings grew colder, fewer hobos crawled out from beneath the elevated tracks of the railroads along Trent. Vickie glanced at her fellow riders, mostly women headed for downtown offices. Immediately she thought of the murder that had been on the news. A young woman had stepped off a downtown bus and was never seen alive again.

She shook her head and surveyed the crowded bus. Quite a few of the women had taken to wearing Christmas corsages on their coat lapels. Vickie thought she might buy herself a sprig of artificial pine trimmed with glitter and red ribbon. She would look for the corsage only if she had time after the main errand of the lunch hour—phoning Joey Parker. At that thought a smile softened her features. Vickie was not one of the popular girls, not one of the girls Joey usually went for. She would always be just outside of that golden circle. While the popular girls wore their hair in the sleek bouffant style of Jackie Kennedy, Vickie's dark locks erupted into loose waves and curls; her skirts were a shade too long to be fashionable, as Gram insisted on hemming them to cover Vickie Lynn's knees. That she was not one of the popular girls made Joey's attention that much more exciting.

Vickie gathered her purse and lunch sack and murmured, "Goodbye" to the driver. She tucked her chin into her woolen neck scarf and walked beneath swags of greenery and red plastic bells swinging in the wind above Riverside Avenue. At the front doors of the aging Zukor Building she stopped at the newsstand opposite the elevators. The front page of the morning paper reported more details of the murder. No one claimed to have seen the young woman after she exited the bus at Post and Riverside. She had been strangled with her own neck scarf. Vickie shivered as she handed Harvey her coins for a package of chewing gum.

"You be careful, missy. That evil-doer would like a young one like you." Harvey nodded towards the headline and displayed his yellowing teeth.

Vickie smiled weakly and made a beeline for the elevator.

At precisely 11:28 Elsie Schumacher entered the partitioned space that sheltered the phone board and donned the second head set. She nodded to indicate that Vickie could unplug her head set to take her lunch break. Vickie mouthed a "thank you" and tried not to smile as Elsie answered her first call. Being a three-pack-a-day smoker, Elsie spoke an octave lower than Vickie. Elsie found it highly insulting when callers mistook her for a man. Vickie hurried to the break room with her lunch sack.

Even though Vickie huddled in a corner seat, Warren Heimbigner still found her. He pushed up his glasses and shifted from foot to foot beside Vickie's chair.

"M-may I sit down?"

Vickie shrugged.

"Th-th-thanks," he stuttered. He took a sandwich out of his lunch sack and removed the wax paper wrapping, folding it with neat creases.

"Do you like movies?" He peered through his thick lenses.

"I guess so." Vickie stared at the remains of her lunch and sighed. Sooner or later she would have to go out with him just to get him out of her hair.

"A musical is playing at the Garland Theater. We could attend this weekend."

Vickie picked up her sandwich bag. "I'll have to check with my grandmother," she said.

Warren nodded. "Of course."

Vickie deposited her uneaten lunch in the trash and left without a backwards glance. Gram would probably classify Warren as a good date. He was polite, held a steady job and wasn't a drinker.

She practically ran all the way to Travo's Restaurant, a place she was fairly certain not to meet any coworkers. She entered the phone booth, dropped in her dime and dialed the number from memory.

"Parker's," a man answered over the noise of automotive tools.

"I'd like to speak to Joey, please."

Muffled sounds came through the receiver as the man shouted, "Joey! It's one of your girlfriends!"

A moment passed then a voice said, "Joey here."

"Hi, it's me."

"Hi, Vic."

Jocy was the only one who called her Vic.

"You want to go to a party tonight?" he asked. "A buddy of mine is on leave from the army."

"Gram will...I mean...yes, that would be great."

"I'll pick you up at seven. See ya."

Her eyes shone as she hung up and hurried through the wind to Newberry's where she found the perfect corsage. When she returned to the Zukor Building, Harvey nodded to her and said, "You're looking very nice and festive."

"Thank you," Vickie replied.

He kept his eyes fastened on her until the elevator doors swallowed her up.

Vickie sat down at the wobbly dining room table where Gram customarily served dinner.

"I'm going to a travelogue on Europe tonight," she said brightly.

Gram set baked beans on the table and smoothed her dress.

"You're not going alone are you?"

"No, I'm getting a ride from Denise at work," Vickie lied.

"It's good for you girls to improve yourselves."

They ate quietly. Vickie cleared the table and washed up the dishes while Gram settled into her wing chair to watch Lawrence Welk.

At five minutes to seven Vickie slipped into the bathroom where she applied black eyeliner and frosted lipstick. She rolled up the waistband of her skirt to shorten it by five inches and then threw on her car coat and ran to the curb. She glanced over her shoulder at the curtained windows and stamped her feet to keep warm until Joey's Plymouth pulled up.

Vickie hopped in and slid across the front seat. Joey gave her a squeeze as he expertly steered the Plymouth with one hand. They sped south through town.

"We're celebrating with Rich. He's got another week before he has to report. They're sending him to Nam."

"Oh," Vickie smiled and leaned her head on Joey's shoulder.

They parked on Sixth and entered an old brick building. Music was blaring from a rear apartment.

"Hey, Joey!" A young man grasped Joey's hand.

Joey grinned and punched his shoulder playfully. "Rich, you son of a gun, this is Vic."

Vickie smiled and nodded. The two boys walked toward the kitchen. Vickie stood in the entryway for a moment and then squeezed onto a low couch next to two other girls. By the time she had folded her car coat, a wiry boy with glasses had pressed a glass of punch into her hands. He said something she couldn't hear over the music and walked away.

Like most parties, this one had promised more fun than it delivered. By nine o'clock Vickie knew she needed to get home. She realized that she hadn't seen Joey in awhile. She pushed her way to the kitchen.

"Where's Joey?" she asked.

"Uh-oh!" the wiry boy exclaimed. Several of the young men hid smiles. In confusion Vickie turned to leave the room. Rich inclined his head towards a door off the kitchen hallway. Vickie walked to the door and peeked in. A dark flush spread upwards from her throat as she caught a glimpse of Joey and a scantily clad girl writhing on a chaise lounge.

Head down, she pulled on her coat and left the apartment. She was almost to the corner when a hand grabbed her elbow.

"You shouldn't walk home alone," Rich said.

"I'm just going to the bus." Vickie was fighting back tears.

Rich stepped closer and looked into her face. "You shouldn't walk by yourself," he repeated.

He threw his arm around her neck, and they lurched forward a few steps. Vickie shrugged herself free.

"I can get to the bus."

She took off at a trot while Rich stood watching with his hands in his pockets. Vickie wrapped her wool scarf tight and quickly covered the blocks to the city center. There was little traffic and only the occasional pedestrian huddled against the cold. Even the overhead decorations seemed forlorn. As the cold air cleared her head, she stopped crying and became angry. She resolved never to see Joey again. She couldn't believe she'd been so stupid as to believe that she was special to him.

At last she could see the marquee of the Post Street Theater. A double feature was just letting out, and it was comforting to have people walking nearby.

"V-V-Vickie?" a familiar voice asked.

She turned to see Warren Heimbigner approaching. She hadn't noticed him in the crowd, but after all, nobody ever noticed Warren.

"Hi, Warren."

"Did you just see the show?"

"No, I'm just waiting for the bus."

Warren drew his brows together and spoke solemnly, "I believe there's only one more bus run this evening. It's not good for you to wait alone. I could give you a ride. My car's just around the corner."

Vickie bit her lip. She glanced at her watch and said, "Okay, if it's not out of your way. I live north of Gonzaga."

"I'm heading north," Warren replied.

They walked silently to his Nash Rambler and Warren opened the passenger door. A pine scented air freshener hung in the window and the bench seat was covered neatly with a plaid stadium blanket. Vickie leaned back and closed her eyes as Warren pulled out onto Trent Avenue.

"I must say that I'm surprised that you are out alone at night," Warren said as he drove. "You seem like a respectable and careful girl."

Vickie gave a short laugh. "I didn't start out alone. The guy I was with wasn't looking for a good girl."

Warren gazed at her through his thick lenses. "Then he wasn't very smart."

He turned his attention back to driving. "I knew what kind of girl you were as soon as you started working the phones."

Vickie shifted uneasily.

"I'd be proud to take you home to meet mother," Warren said. "Would you mind?"

Vickie looked at him in surprise. "You mean now? I really need to get home soon or Gram will worry."

"It will only take a few minutes."

"I guess so," she said without enthusiasm.

Vickie looked out at the lights decorating the windows and rooftops of the century-old homes as Warren drove west. He pulled to the curb in front of a neat, white craftsman house. The curtains were parted to show the tree in the window. He helped her out and they walked up the front steps and into a dark entryway. Warren switched on a light and guided Vickie into the room.

She took in the quaint loveseat and chair decorated with crocheted doilies and then gave a little gasp. Blue knitted slippers were set in front of a rocking chair. The side table held a teacup and plate. A shawl was draped across the back of the chair on which rested a covered brass urn.

Warren addressed the urn, "Mother, this is Vickie, the girl I told you about. I can assure you that she's a respectable girl." He looked expectantly at Vickie.

She licked her lips and breathed rapidly. "I... ah...hello," she said faintly.

Warren leaned towards the rocker and Vickie inched backwards towards the door. She had the knob in her hand when Warren grabbed her scarf.

"Don't insult Mother," he said.

Vickie knew she should think of something to say and walk out, but fatigue and alcohol caught up with her. She began to laugh.

"Stop, stop!" Warren cried.

Warren pulled the scarf tighter. Vickie's laughter turned to screams.

"Vickie, don't! The neighbors will hear! I can't believe this is happening again!"

Vickie's screaming grew weaker and then stopped as the scarf cut off all air. Her body slid to the floor.

"Now I have to find another good girl to meet Mother," Warren wailed as he reached down and adjusted her skirt to cover her knees.

Indecision
By Mark Shilo

It was Saturday and going to be a beautiful day after a week of rain. Or was it? Robert looked down again. It lay there still, quiet in the early spring morning sun, as if it had popped up like some kind of mushroom. Robert tried to think, but it was difficult. Perhaps it was some kind of silly gag, he thought.

A human arm lay on the front steps mat like the morning paper. The arm was tanned and bare. It appeared to be from a younger person, gender not clear, tending towards a medium or slight build. Flesh and bone were visible at the meaty end where the arm would have attached to the shoulder. The arm did not seem all that ghastly. It was very clean, as if it had just been delivered fresh from some neighborhood meat counter. Robert continued to stare down. There was only the smallest hint of blood oozing at the severed end, which otherwise appeared to be drying out.

Robert suddenly closed the door. This was most disturbing. He must call the police at once. But then he wondered—was it genuine, a real arm? What if this were some dreadful joke? What a poor one! he thought. But that arm did look quite vivid. He could see it now in his mind, lying there.

Robert stood behind the door a few moments, opened it again slightly, then closed it once more and shuffled to the telephone, glancing cautiously over his shoulder back towards the front door. As he reached the telephone by the couch, he half expected some disconnected hand to appear and start dialing. For some reason he stopped. What if there were other...things...like this lying around in his yard outside? He might fall under suspicion.

These things just don't magically fall out of the sky, he thought. Someone puts them there. Someone who wanted to cause trouble for him.

A vague sense of uneasiness and fear descended upon him. As always, he knew, he would not be able to think or decide anything now.

It was too real to be a joke, he thought as his head began to clear at last somewhat. But then what? He could not pick up the phone. He hated this feeling of such terrible dread and fear. He knew those feelings, his companions in a way, he thought. And he knew as always, in the end, that things were going be his fault. He turned back and opened the door, looking carefully at the arm, then up and down the street. It was so early still, he reflected. No cars, no one else up. Maybe the paper boy would come though. Had he come? Robert did not see the paper. It was still early, must be only about 5:30 or so. But the paper would come soon he knew.

And then it came to him with a jolt. Someone must be scoping him on a telescopic camera. It would surely just now be poking through the slats of a neighbor's window blinds. The arm was a wax dummy, and at this moment he was being filmed, he thought—more rapidly now—for "The World's Funniest Videos." But it wasn't funny at all.

Robert realized immediately that he was becoming quite queasy. He felt a little bend in his knees, and then he was uncontrollably retching from the depths of his body, not managing even to save his dignity by closing the door. How awful it had all become. But it was always like that, he thought. He was always the one to be caught and embarrassed. Everyone thought it was so funny to make him the dunce. He wanted to shout, but could not. He could not shut out the picture from his childhood reader of the bad boy in the corner with the tall dunce hat. How he hated that picture.

Robert felt his face grow pale and cool, then darken. It was a deep anger. He had had the feeling before. And then, it was odd, very odd that he felt nothing at all. He watched himself open the door once more in a sweeping motion with one hand. He picked the arm up by the heavier end and swung it quickly inside. The tips of the dead fingers brushed so gently in the small puddle of retch that had spilled along the threshold. How stiff it was, like a dead cat, but much heavier than he'd imagined.

Robert shut the door firmly and dropped the arm in the front door hallway by the coat closet. How loud the thud was. For no reason he could tell, his eyes were now stinging with tears. He saw himself collapse. He could hear his breathing, difficult and gulping as he sobbed. How very detached he was, he thought, feeling nothing as he wept uncontrollably.

At last, Robert's heaving chest slowed. He picked up the arm, then set it down. What was he doing now? At last, he rose slowly. He saw that his pants were soiled, smelling of vomit and faintly, blood. A little drink would be good, he thought. Leaving the arm and vomit, Robert walked with a not quite regular step into the kitchen and poured out a small glass of Kesslers blend whiskey, neat. He set the glass on the kitchen table and sat down. He needed to think. The whiskey would help. He sipped it. How nice it felt, so warm going down.

Soon, the glow of the liquor raised his spirits. It would be OK now, he thought. Those hard feelings of fear, embarrassment and shame seemed to grow more distant now. Into the toaster popped the wonderful "Thomas" sourdough English muffins; "the original nooks and crannies muffins," said the label. Robert knew he should read labels. Just another touch of Kesslers, he thought, and then his head would clear. He would feel better, steady.

Robert felt he was now moving back many years and decades to his boyhood. How he loved to go there, to the protected and loving home and the secure Christian upbringing.

Deeper his mind wandered to the sunny days of youth. He heard quite clearly in his mind the soft clink clink of milk bottles from the back porch steps. It was the milkman delivering the milk, he realized suddenly. We must rush to catch him! What a wonderful cap and uniform he had, with resplendent yellow jacket and cap, and "Darigold" in fancy red stitching on the vest. The thin gray and white vertical striped pants were immaculate.

He carried an open wire cage with a half dozen gleaming fresh glass quart bottles and a few other things. The milkman had already picked up the empties left in the wire bottle case on the back porch and replaced them with full bottles. Robert thought of his own boyhood toy milk bottle case with white painted milk bottles. They were wooden and smaller. How grand it was to carry them about the house and deliver the milk.

The real delivery happened very quickly. Mother would be cooking and just barely have time to open the back door as the milkman was leaving. She would say, "How about a pint of your cottage cheese?" And he would already be handing it up, always ready, he was. Sometimes though, he would have to whisk back to the shiny red and yellow truck parked out in front. It had a little vertical folding door like a tiny bus. It opened on the curb side so the man could hop in and out to grab something. Then he was gone.

The thoughts were gone then. Collecting himself back to the present, Robert looked at the arm on the floor. He was alone. He didn't want the arm, didn't want to think about it. But he must act. He must take charge of this thing. He picked up the arm, which was surprisingly heavy, and carried it to the kitchen sink. Turning the water on, he began washing it and examining it closely, as if to learn some hidden secret. It needs washing, he thought, as it likely had many germs on it. But it was big and awkward. There was his big bread knife, and soon he was cutting and chopping. He worked in silence, his brow knitted in thought. Was it a dream? he wondered. It was hard work, but he felt very automatic, robotic as he watched himself. He could feel nothing now, except perhaps a strange, sweet arousal. There was something physical about it, he realized. How ashamed he was then, but he could not help himself.

As he continued his exertions, the effort combined with the liquor somehow relaxed him, and he began to feel better again. The remains had become quite slippery now, and Robert saw also that he had cut his own hand by accident. It was not serious, but this added to the soothing feelings somehow, and even a feeling of release. It had all been so very stressful, he realized. Robert set what was left of the arm down, squirted a bit of dish detergent on his hands and cleansed himself. Drying his hands on the dishtowel, he walked back to the living room couch, stretched out and was soon asleep.

How long later he did not know, he was awakened by the telephone. There was Nancy, his baby sister. She was a college student in her second year at Whitworth, in Spokane. "Hi, Bubbles!" she said brightly. She was always at ease, so charming and caring.

Not like me, Robert thought.

As always, Robert struggled to reply. He managed finally, "Hey, Nance. Beautiful day. What's it like in Spokane?" He heard himself speaking a little too loudly. Why was he doing that? He might make her suspicious or something. He noticed then a slender half fingernail sticking on the front of his shirt. He had to get off the phone. But she kept talking. He was trapped. As she continued, Robert carried the cordless back to the sink, inspecting it sharply, along with the counter and floor of the surrounding area. He concentrated to assure himself there were no other errant scraps. It all urgently needed to stay contained inside the sink, he thought. It was terrible to have to listen to Nancy and sound nonchalant, interested, etc. How strange that there was no blood. He had thought that there should be more.

"So when are you coming to visit, Bubbles?" she asked. "You said you would you know, and now that you've been laid off, you have *no* excuses!" She continued as he listened silently, "Come on, Robert!" She always called him that when she was trying to be serious—something difficult for Nancy, Robert thought. She chattered on, he half listening, responding with mono-syllables. He tried again to think of things to say, but it was always the same questions for him. Your subjects? Boyfriends? Doing anything fun? What's the weather like? It trickled out, the same memorized pattern. It was all he knew.

She hadn't been able to reach Mom. (Their father was now deceased.) Could Robert mention to Mother that she needed an extra $200 for books? And they were raising her rent $50? "Love you Bubbles," she said at last.

"You too Nance," came his ready answer. Could she hear he was anxious? It had been less than ten minutes, but finally, as the phone call finished, Robert felt an immense sense of relief.

Spokane. He'd been there once, he remembered now, when the family had dropped Nancy off after traveling from their home in Oak Harbor. A dumb city. "Whitworth"? Sounded like some stuffy English fart, Robert imagined, half smiling.

Staring now at the sink, Robert took the shreds of flesh, tendon, and bone and wrapped them in clear plastic in one, two, three, four layers for good measure. Then he rolled the lumpy bundle carefully in newspaper. What to do now? He thought of Arthur Simpson, his old work associate. He did not like Simpson. It had been one of his happiest days at the job when "Buck" Simpson finally retired. Simpson was always sure to make a joke about him, always sure to tease or ridicule. But then, unfortunately, Robert had been laid off himself just a few weeks later. The firm had fallen on hard times and had to downsize. Just as things were going to be better, he had to find a new job. It was always like that, Robert knew.

But now, Robert finally began to feel himself under control. He carefully wiped up the vomit with a yellow dish towel and then wrapped the towel around the newspaper. He found an old box he had saved and stuffed the dish toweled bundle in the box, covering it carefully with grocery sack paper. Then he taped it all securely and in neat, careful block letters he addressed the package to his old supervisor "Michael Saunders," for whom he also had no great feelings of affection, making sure the return address was carefully shown to be from Arthur Simpson. He moved quickly to his car and drove to the mailbox in front of Walgreen's, down the street. The package was quickly mailed, and Robert was relieved. Had he waited at all, rather than acting on impulse, he knew he would have never done it.

Later that afternoon, Robert was quite surprised to open his car trunk and see the rest of the body. It came back to him then, but only in partial memory, as in a dream. The person had wanted a ride, and there was something about them. They were so vulnerable somehow. And they would not shut up, talking on and on so incessantly. Robert was the nervous sort, he knew.

He didn't always manage well with people who were too friendly. They usually wanted something. They would not leave you alone.

And so, much later, after dark, Robert saw himself driving to a lonely area along the bay a few miles down the road from town. The water was deep there when the tide came in, and the road led very close to a small cliff overlooking the sound. It was a good place, he knew, to get rid of things.

The next day dawned warm and sunny again. Another beautiful morning. Nothing on the porch today, Robert noted. But then he saw a very small dark spot where the arm had been. Just a little blood spot, he knew. Might have come from a bad cut or something—it was nothing to worry about, even though he needed to be more careful. Definitely, he had been careless. It must never happen like that again.

He felt the warm spring sun pleasant on his shoulders and neck. He needed to get away, really get entirely out. What about Spokane? Maybe a new start, a new town would help him get his mind off the things he wanted to forget, wanted to leave behind forever. Nancy actually liked Spokane quite a lot. Could he find work there? He needed to think this through a little more. But it was always so hard for him to decide things when he had to think about them. Better for him to just act on impulse. He hated it so when he was undecided.

Work Ethic
By Steve Oliver

Carl looked up from his work with a start. He had heard a noise outside, the slam of a car door he thought. He leaned a little to his left so he could see more clearly out of the second story window. A small car had parked at the entrance to the long driveway leading to his country house. He carefully put his tools down and jogged downstairs to the kitchen. He quickly washed up and was drying his hands with an old towel as he stepped out of the sun porch door onto his deck. He surveyed the property quickly. It was a rural scene, a five acre paradise, graced with many pine trees, decorative shrubs and, of course, the flower beds, constantly watched over and groomed by his wife Sara. Everything looked in order except for the nondescript little green Japanese car that now blocked the drive.

Cars seldom came into the driveway. People traveling on the paved county road were usually on their way to a local landfill or were taking a short-cut to the airport. Most of them didn't pay much attention to the houses that lined the road on their way. It was all the more reason to be apprehensive about a car showing up unannounced.

Carl headed down the driveway, studying the car, looking for its occupants and its reason for stopping. He saw that the driver and passenger seats were empty, but after a moment he could see movement at the back of the car. The small trunk was open and he could see the tops of two heads.

"Hi there," said Carl, loud enough to get their attention from a distance.

A young man stepped into view. He smiled. "Hi," he said.

"What's up?" asked Carl, but he wanted to say *What the are you doing in my driveway?*

The guy was young, maybe twenty-two, Mexican or one of the other groups they referred to as Hispanic. He was a nice-looking kid, very muscular, wearing tan shorts and a black t-shirt. "We had a flat," he said. "Just coming up the hill."

Carl nodded, staying where he was, not wanting to come any closer. He had heard in recent years about home invasion robberies and he didn't want to be a victim. He seldom had visits from strangers and he didn't think this was a robbery, but there was no point in taking the chance.

"So you've got it under control, then?" he said, hoping that was the case.

"Yeah, we'll get it changed," said the man.

Carl was about to leave when the other man appeared from behind the car. His appearance startled Carl a little because he was a fat, black guy wearing a baseball cap sideways. Together the two guys fit Carl's picture of a pair of gang members, the kind who shot kids standing on the curb for no good reason, or broke into a home in the country for money for drugs. The fat kid not only had the baseball cap and t-shirt, but also the long, baggy shorts that were popular with gang-bangers, as well as a big pair of what Carl would have called sneakers. The kid didn't have a gun or a club in his hand, but Carl still saw him as a threat.

"Well, I'll leave you to it, then," he said, retreating casually to the house. "Let me know if you need any help."

The Mexican kid waved in acknowledgement, and Carl went back into the house by the sliding door. Once inside he locked it and trotted up the stairs to the master bedroom where he opened the drawer to the night stand. He took the holstered .38 out of the drawer, pulled up his shirt and put the flap of the holster behind his belt to secure it. He put the shirt back in place and decided that it looked okay, like he had something under there, but perhaps they wouldn't be able to tell that it was a gun. It was just a precaution anyway, as they would soon be done and on their way—this was just in case they were up to something, he would not be completely helpless.

He decided that he didn't want to resume his work while they were outside, so he went downstairs and put on water for coffee and turned on the radio. He sat at the table and re-read the morning paper. When the coffee was ready, he drank it and read the paper again and listened to the guy on talk radio who said things Carl agreed with. Occasionally he walked to the window on the sun porch and peered out the driveway to see if the car was still there. The third time he did this he became concerned when he saw that the car had not moved.

He turned the radio off, checked that his gun was not showing, and headed down the driveway once more.

The car was parked where it had been when he had first seen it. It was not jacked up, and the front driver's side tire was as flat as a flitter.

What bothered Carl more than the flat tire was the sight of the two men both sitting in the front seats, both appearing to be napping.

Without coming too close to the car he called, "What's happening?"

The Mexican kid brought his seat to an upright position and climbed out of the car. The black guy stirred and looked at him, but didn't get out.

"We don't have a jack," he said. He pulled out his cell phone and started dialing. "I've been trying to reach a friend to see if he has a jack."

Carl was a little alarmed now. Was this a ploy to get him closer to the car where they could overpower him? How could that be if the black guy was going to sleep in his seat the whole time?

"You need a jack, huh? What does that take— just a small scissors jack?"

"I dunno." The Mexican kid shrugged.

"Wait there," said Carl. "I'll see what I can find." He headed toward his pickup, thinking about the type of jack he had and whether it would likely fit the little car. He had never had to use it so wasn't sure even that it was the right type.

He managed to get the jack from its holder under the seat and took it to the car. He hoped to hand it to the Mexican kid from as great a distance as he could manage and then hoped the kid would know what to do with it. The kid took it, but after that the results weren't too promising.

The jack was supposed to be placed perpendicular to the car under the front part of the body, by the driver's door. There would be a notch where it was to fit and the fitting for the handle could then be turned and the car lifted.

But the Mexican kid was putting the jack under the car in a way that was completely wrong. First, he put it parallel to the car. When Carl had said, "No, not that way," he had turned it so that the fitting was underneath the car, just opposite the way it went.

Carl was startled by the voice of the other man, the black kid, who had gotten out of the car and now stood uncomfortably close to him on his left. "Turn it around the other way," he said to the Mexican kid.

The kid turned it the other way and Carl backed up a bit to give himself maneuvering room. He was worried that his pistol would do him very little good at such close range unless he was lucky enough to get it out of the holster fast.

"It won't go into the slot," said the Mexican kid. "The car's too low."

"I'll lift it," said the black kid. He pulled up on the car by the front bumper, lifting the body several inches higher at the front. The Mexican kid managed to get the jack into place and Carl handed him the jack handle. Carl couldn't quite believe the trouble the kid had with it. He kept choosing the wrong thing to attach to the jack's fitting. First he tried to turn it by using the cylindrical end of one of the jack's coupling links. Then he put the link into it sideways. Finally both Carl and the black kid were trying to grab at the jack handle to show the Mexican the proper end to use on the fitting. Even after he managed to get the right connection to the jack the kid didn't seem to know how to turn it right. Both Carl and the black kid seemed to know how to do it, but the Mexican kid was the one with the handle.

Carl was totally engrossed in watching the Mexican kid handle the jack when he felt a hand on his shoulder. He jumped back with a start.

It was the black kid's hand. When Carl reacted, he let go, but still leaned his face toward Carl's.

"You believe how dumb he is?" he asked.

Carl shook his head. He was in agreement, but he didn't want the black kid this close to him. What if this was a ruse? Maybe the Mexican kid wasn't that stupid.

The black kid backed away again and went on telling the other guy how to do his work.

After what seemed like half an hour, they had the car off the ground. Carl had had to advise the kid on everything—that he needed to loosen the lug nut before getting the tire off the ground, that he needed to turn the nuts counter-clockwise to loosen them, that the lug wrench would not work unless the fitting was snug on the nut. The guy was nice-looking and well-built, giving the impression he was above average, but he didn't seem smart enough to tie his shoes. What was that about? The black guy looked like trailer park trash who had been over-eating his whole life, but he could have done the job in half the time. And through all this Carl kept waiting for the other shoe to drop, for one of them to attack him, grab for the gun that seemed all too obvious now.

By the time the new spare—not a spare at all, but one of the little, hard-rubber phony tires the cars carried these days, was finally on the car and secured with lug nuts, Carl was about half out of his mind with frustration and worry. As the two kids loaded up their tools, Carl still worried that this had all been a ruse. Perhaps they would, at the last minute, still attack him, or perhaps they would come back in an hour or a day, now knowing the layout of the place, and break in.

They took so long getting packed up that Carl finally lost patience. He said, "Good luck on your trip. I've got work to do."

The boys thanked him and waved as he walked back to the house. He locked the door and made another cup of coffee while he kept an eye on them. Finally, they got in the car and backed out of the driveway.

Carl hurried to the other side of the house and looked out the window at his other driveway, where he had a view of the road heading toward the airport. If these kids had been telling the truth, that's the way they would be going. He wanted to confirm that they were leaving, that they were finally on their way.

Carl waited long enough that he was beginning to worry that this was a trick when he finally saw the car pass. The Mexican kid was driving and the black kid appeared to be sleeping in the passenger seat.

Carl stood at the window for ten minutes or more, watching to see if they doubled back. Then he went to the kitchen and stood for awhile, occasionally taking a sip of the now-cold coffee. Finally, he put the cup on the table. He looked up at the ceiling as if he could see his work still waiting for him upstairs.

He washed his hands and rolled up his sleeves and trudged up the stairs to the master bedroom. There on the bed lay the body of his wife, Sara, half naked on a small blue tarp. Next to her on an oilcloth were his butchering tools—mainly various knives and saws, along with a roll of paper towels and some rags.

"Well," he said, in a tone that Sara had often used when encouraging him to do work that needed to be done, "This work won't get done by itself."

He picked up a saw and started in.

The Skating Party
By Barbara Curtis

I have no recollection of the evening of December the twenty-first. I know that Trinity Church had a Christmas pageant, because I directed it. I suppose the angels sang in tune and the kings entered on cue bearing gifts, but I could not tell you one single thing about the performance if my life depended on it. My brain was on temporary overload from the events of the day. December the twenty-first was the day that I killed the man who raped my daughter.

I use the word raped because it conveys the true meaning of the act much better than molested—a quaint word describing behavior that is marginally unacceptable. Marcie was raped by her Bible School teacher when she was twelve years old.

Her attacker was one William Renford, a slender man with thick blonde hair. He was thirty-eight years old at the time and had been raping young girls for twenty-two years. We all knew him as Will, a soft-spoken man always willing to lend a hand. No one thought it odd that he wasn't married. Will was devoted to his faith—nearly like a priest.

A week before that fateful December day I was in the church basement setting up for a luncheon when Will came down the stairs.

"Let me help you with that, Mrs. Lindstrom," he said.

We stood at opposite ends of a folding table and smoothed out a white table cloth.

"I'd like to take the kids to the Ice Palace Sunday afternoon. It will be my treat, kind of an early Christmas present," he said.

"That's very nice, Will. I'm sure Marcie will want to go."

He smiled and we moved to the next table.

"I could go with you if you need help supervising," I offered.

"That won't be necessary. You enjoy an afternoon by yourself," he replied.

"That sounds pretty tempting," I said.

I walked into the kitchen as my fellow volunteers continued a conversation that had started without me.

"The slime ball seems to know the law," said Charlie Donahue as he sipped his coffee and helped himself to a donut. "He didn't touch the girl until she was twelve; makes a difference."

"I'm not sure I believe any of it," said Margaret Betz. "He's on the library board and serves as a deacon at his church."

"Are you talking about the guy from Loon Lake?" I asked.

Charlie nodded. He pointed his sausage-shaped finger at Margaret. "The reason you don't believe it is that by the time this got to court, the girl had grown up. You see a mature seventeen-year-old. I bet she didn't look like that at twelve."

"I don't know. I just think she would have told her parents if there was anything inappropriate going on," Margaret said. "And he seems like such a nice man."

"They always do," Charlie muttered as Margaret carried the coffee urn out to the serving table.

"I guess you have a different view of things," I said, reaching for a donut.

"Thirty years as a cop will do that to you," he said. "I'll tell you one thing—if I knew a sicko like that had touched my daughter, I don't know that I'd waste time with the lawyers and courts."

I looked him in the eye. "You're serious."

"Yes, I'm serious."

"I'd like to think that you wouldn't be able to do that," I said.

"Everybody has the capacity to kill, Roberta, even you."

It turned out Charlie was right.

On Sunday, Will took the kids to the Ice Palace. Marcie got home at nine, took her skates to her room and shut the door. A half hour later she emerged dressed in flannel pajamas and said tearfully, "Mom, I have to tell you something."

I tried to keep the panic from showing as Marcie explained how Renford had started giving her extra attention in Bible Group last year. She proceeded to tell me how he had taught her to "experience God's love" over the past six months. She pulled her knees up and rested her chin on them to whisper, "He told me I was special and grown up. He made me do things. He said it was our special secret because other people just wouldn't understand. I really believed him."

"He knew you would believe him because you're young, and he knew you were respectful of adults." My voice was calm but my stomach churned.

"Ever since my birthday he's been spending a lot of time with Kelly Jo. He ignored me tonight and talked to her instead. She's only twelve, and I think he's saying the same things to her. I feel so stupid!"

"Oh, honey." I opened my arms and Marcie sat on my lap like she used to when she was six. We hugged and cried. "I'll take care of things," I whispered into her soft hair.

After Marcie went to bed I sat in the living room without bothering to turn on the lights. By two a.m. the pain had moved from my stomach to my chest. I covered myself with a blanket and got a few hours of sleep.

At dawn I staggered into the bathroom and stared into the mirror. My reflection didn't seem much different, but I knew that the person looking back now was not the person whose image I'd seen yesterday. I showered and dressed and woke Marcie. I fixed breakfast just like a normal person, but I wasn't able to eat. Coffee and aspirin cleared my head enough to drive Marcie to school and head for Trinity Church.

I knocked on the door to the pastor's study and waited.

"I don't believe Reverend Daniels is in, Miz Lindstrom."

"Oh, hello, Ed. Do you know when he'll be back?"

The old custodian shook his head and leaned forward to give me a closer look.

"Pardon my saying, but you look all in. Why don't you sit down while you wait."

"No thanks, I'll come back later."

"Miz Lindstrom, if you got troubles you should pray." He reached out a gnarled hand and touched my arm. "I've had me a lot of troubles in my day and there wasn't nothing prayer couldn't fix."

I smiled sadly. "I don't think prayer can fix my problem."

Ed shook his head of curly white hair.

"People nowadays don't understand the power of prayer. You see, prayer is the strongest force there is. You spend some time on your knees, and you'll have all the power of heaven and earth at your disposal."

He gave my arm a final pat and began his bow-legged walk down the hallway.

I headed across the hall to the church office. As a member of the pastoral council it wasn't unusual for me to drop in.

The church secretary smiled and said, "Good morning, Roberta."

"Good morning, Betty. I need to pull something from the council files. I won't be a minute."

"Call me if you need help."

I walked to the tiny back room and scanned the file cabinets, keeping an ear tuned to the outer office. Within two minutes I had pulled the personal information card on William Renford. It listed his mother in North Bend as his emergency contact. I copied her phone number and pushed the drawer shut.

Betty was on the phone and mouthed a silent goodbye to me as I walked out the door.

At home, I drank another cup of coffee before I punched in the phone number. I was about to cut off Will Renford's support line before I pressed charges.

"Hello?" an elderly voice queried.

"Mrs. Renford, I'm calling from Spokane, from the Trinity Church Council."

"Who? You're calling from Spokane?"

"I'm a church council member. I want to prepare you for some bad news regarding your son."

"I suppose it's some girl trying to get William into trouble again, just because he's so good looking and such a nice boy."

"Again?"

"Ever since high school these girls have been after him. One little tramp even said she had his baby. Ridiculous!"

"I didn't know...." I stammered.

"You just tell that slut that my William is a good boy who takes care of his mother!"

She hung up.

I stared out at the gray December sky for a long time. Finally I roused myself and walked down the basement steps. The bare bulb threw weak light onto the shelves at the far wall. I reached toward the back of the deep shelf and pulled out a wooden box. I set it on the floor and lifted the lid. Wrapped in a cloth bag was Papa's .38 revolver, still smelling faintly of oil. In a box next to it were the bullets. I fumbled with the cylinder release awhile before it popped open and I was able to slip six bullets into place. The gun seemed to be in working order, but I really couldn't be sure until the time came to use it.

The revolver felt incredibly heavy when I carried it upstairs and placed it in the pocket of my ski jacket. By the time Marcie got home from school the box was back in its dark corner, and I was baking cookies.

The phone rang as I was taking the last batch out of the oven. It was my mother.

After a few minutes of stilted conversation she asked, "Roberta, what's wrong?"

"Nothing."

"Don't tell me nothing's wrong. I've been your mother too long for that. I can hear it in your voice."

Silence stretched between us. I broke it quietly.

"Mom, If I were hospitalized or had a long illness, would you stay with Marcie?"

"Oh, no! What's wrong?"

"Nothing is wrong. You know how it is. Sometimes you starting thinking *what if*. I was just dwelling on what if something happened that I couldn't take care of Marcie. You'd take care of her, wouldn't you?"

"Of course I would. You shouldn't worry about that. Are you all right?"

"Yes, Mom. I'm sorry I worried you with it. Maybe you can talk to me about it some more this weekend."

"Of course I will. I'll be sending you warm thoughts, sweetheart. Be sure to call me."

"Thanks, Mom."

I broke the connection and put my head down on the kitchen table. After awhile, I sat up and began to plan the script for the finest piece of acting I'd ever attempt.

The following night, I arranged to be in the church foyer when the Men's Prayer Group meeting let out. Blood roared in my ears and I felt dizzy, but I remembered my script; I forced myself to look at Renford and to pull my lips into a smile.

"Will, can you meet me Saturday morning for a quick trip to Twin Lakes? I'd like to show you an ice-skating spot where you could take the Bible School kids. I know it from years ago. It's a great place for a cook-out."

"I guess so," he said doubtfully.

"I'll show you how to get there so that you can take the kids by yourself."

"I believe I can make time for that," he said.

"You'll love it," I said with as much enthusiasm as I could muster.

"Do you mind if we drive separately? I need to go to the Outlet Mall in Post Falls afterwards." The idea of sitting in the car with Renford made me nauseous.

He shrugged. "Okay."

"Meet me in front of the church at nine and bring your skates."

"I'll do that. Good night, Mrs. Lindstrom."

"Good night," I said and watched him exit the building.

As soon as he was out of sight I collapsed into a nearby chair.

At eight-thirty Saturday morning, I dropped Marcie off at Karen's house for the day. As she carried her bag of board games up the walk, I studied her coltish legs, flat chest and bobbing ponytail, and I cursed Will Renford with renewed vigor.

Sunglasses hid my eyes when I met him in front of the church. I drove east for thirty-five minutes, with Renford following. When we pulled onto the Twin Lakes access road, I reached down to feel the .38 in my coat pocket. We parked and got out into the bright, cold air. My hands shook so that I could hardly lace up my skates.

"The place I have in mind is a cove around the bend from the ice-fishing spot." I pointed down the lake. "The skating is good and there's a fireplace made of natural rock."

I skated off without a look back. Renford followed. I heard him stumble some on the frozen surface. As I had suspected, he was used to skating only at ice rinks.

The cove was sheltered from the wind, and the fireplace was still standing, just as I remembered it.

Renford smiled as he circled the ice. "This will be a super place for a skating party."

"Yes, it will," I agreed.

I had turned away to reach into my coat pocket, feeling for the revolver, when I heard the unmistakable crack of ice breaking.

Renford had skated to the very spot where I knew a stream bubbled into the lake beneath the ice. He didn't know enough to lie down so he dropped into the frigid water, his gloved hands grasping futilely at the ice.

I studied the shoreline to confirm that it was bare of limbs or branches, then skated as near as I dared to the open water and stretched myself out, confirming that I could not reach the struggling man without endangering myself.

I got to my knees and began to pray. I prayed like I've never prayed before, summoning all the power of heaven and earth. Finally, I opened my eyes and said quietly, "Will, it's time to experience God's love."

He was looking at me as his mouth formed a wordless O and he vanished into the icy water.

An hour later, wrapped in a blanket and with the red light of the sheriff's car flashing into my face I recounted my inability to reach Renford and my final, fervent prayer at the edge of the ice. The deputy pushed a cup of steaming coffee into my hands.

"Sit in the car where it's warm, ma'am. You can give a formal statement later. It's too bad your prayers weren't answered."

I didn't bother to correct him.

Payback
By Dan Webster

Jeanette pulled herself straight and admired what she saw in the mirror.

Her breasts pushed against the thin fabric of the blouse, and the jeans hugged her hips. Two years of exercise and Mexican sun had done wonders for a body that had been attractive to begin with.

She threw back her head and shook her blond hair. OK, so it's from a bottle, she thought, but it looks convincing enough to fool Sean.

As if Sean had ever been hard to manipulate.

They went way back, Jeanette and Sean. Back to high school when she was the sexiest cheerleader and he was the star running back. She'd seen him as her way out, and he hadn't disappointed. Not as long as Jeannette had been there to show him what he needed to do.

The first thing had been to dump his old girlfriend, that glasses-wearing geek whom he'd taken to the junior prom. Jeanette had just transferred at the semester break, and she'd spent the first few months checking out the scene, trying to figure out who was who, what was what.

And then at the beginning of senior year, when Jeanette had managed to win a spot on the cheerleading squad—one afternoon alone with her counselor had assured that—she began to see things clearly. It was after that first game, when Sean had rushed for 227 yards and three touchdowns, that she'd made her move.

It had been easy to position herself where the team would run on the field. It had been even easier to step in front of Sean as he ran, head down, toward the sideline. She hadn't liked being knocked down, but the look on his face—surprise, shock, concern—was worth it.

She realized that after the game when he called her. And the next night when he drove to her house. And certainly an hour after that when he was coming in her mouth and moaning that he loved her.

It had been so good that following Monday morning when they walked down the hallway together, hand in hand. The look on the geek's face—surprise, shock, hatred—was priceless. Jeanette merely smiled sweetly, as if her being with Sean had been the most natural thing in the world.

And it seemed to be. The feeling endured throughout the season, when he'd broken records and earned attention from every major college in the nation. It was still strong that spring when he signed a letter of intent with the University of Washington. And even at graduation, when they danced at the prom and pledged to be together forever.

Then the trouble hit. Olivia, Jeanette's mother, began to interfere. Always a drinker, she began hitting the bottle every day. Jeanette would come home, and Olivia would begin. She would say how Jeanette never paid her any respect, that she was just like her no-good father, that she would end up waiting on tables or selling Avon products. Who was Jeanette, Olivia asked, to think that she was going to get out of crummy Spokane?

Then she went too far. She forbade Jeanette to see Sean.

"I know what you two are doing," Olivia said one night, pointing a drunken finger at her daughter. "You're not fooling anyone. And I'm not going to stand for it anymore. Just because your bastard father isn't around doesn't mean you can do just anything you want. I'm going to tell your teachers, I'm going to tell his parents, I'm going to do whatever I can to break you two up."

The older woman smiled. "You just see if I don't," she said.

For the first time in as long as she could remember, Jeanette felt afraid. Things seemed beyond her control. She wasn't sure what to do, but she knew that her mother couldn't be allowed to ruin Jeanette's life as completely as she had her own. So she called Sean.

But first, she made sure her mother was thoroughly drunk. Even as she yelled, Olivia continued to drink. Jeanette forced herself to act contrite, apologizing and promising that she would change, that she would stop seeing Sean. All the while, she continued to fill her mother's glass.

When Olivia passed out, Jeanette called. Sean was clearly concerned, arriving at her house ten minutes later, but he parked a block away as she'd told him to. And he'd come to the back door.

Once inside, he listened as Jeanette told him the whole story. He held her as she cried, telling him how horrible her mother was, how she had driven her father away, how she now threatened to ruin their lives—emphasizing the word *their*—and all because they loved each other. Sean cried, too, thinking that he would lose this girl whom he desperately wanted, and who clearly wanted him.

But he pulled back when she suggested murder.

"It's the only way," Jeanette pleaded, her gorgeous face puffy and smeared with tears. "She'll never let me go otherwise."

"But...but..." Sean stuttered as Jeanette powered on.

"It'll be easy," she said. She explained about her mother's practice of taking a bath every night. How the bathtub was especially big and how easy it would be to put her in it and hold her down. And best of all, Jeanette said, "No one will ever know. They'll just think that she got drunk, passed out and died."

Sean was speechless. Jeanette could tell he thought she was crazy. His eyes told her that this was all a bad dream.

And then Jeanette played her trump card.

"You know," she said, "she'll make sure that you lose your scholarship."

"What?" Sean said. "How can she do that?"

Jeanette looked down. She placed her hands in her lap and said, in a small voice, "She knows that I'm pregnant."

Sean stood and took two steps toward the door. On the other side of that door was the normal world. On the other side of that door he could go back to being what he was.

But Jeanette was ahead of him.

"You'll lose your scholarship, you know," she said. "Mother said she would go to your parents and force you to marry me. And you know what your father would do then."

Sean stood, unmoving.

"He'd make you join the business," Jeanette said. "You'd be back to changing tires. Only this time it would be a career, not just a summer job."

She stepped around in front of him. She took his face in her hands. "But it doesn't have to be like that. We can get rid of the baby. No one ever has to know. Then we both get what we want. And we get it together. All you have to do is help me."

That's how Sean came to carry Jeanette's mother upstairs. He laid her on the bathroom floor and listened to her snore as Jeanette undressed her and then filled the tub. Then he lifted her up, his hands nearly recoiling at the touch of her naked skin, and set her gently in the water. Jeanette directed him to the foot of the tub where he took hold of Olivia's feet. And he held on tight as Jeanette pushed her mother's head under the water.

Olivia came alive almost immediately, twisting and kicking so hard that it was all Sean could do to hold on. She grabbed at Jeanette, trying to push herself up. Jeanette could see her mother's face beneath the water, could see her open eyes glaring up in frustrated rage. She maintained her grip. It was a battle of wills, but Sean was the deciding factor. Good, old, dependable Sean.

Yet it still surprised Jeanette when Olivia, her expression now one of desperation, opened her mouth and coughed out an explosion of bubbles.

She kicked once, twice, and then began a series of convulsive shudders. Gradually, her arms fell limp, and she ceased moving altogether.

Sean let go and stepped back. The room was quiet now. The only sound came from Jeanette, who was moaning—it was almost a keen—as she continued to hold her mother beneath the killing water.

Sean sat on the toilet. He listened to the click of the cooling pipes, the cracks of the old house as it continued to settle on its foundation, the muffled sound of a television set somewhere downstairs. Finally, he reached over and touched Jeanette's arm.

"You can stop now," he said. "It's over."

Jeanette started. She turned to Sean, a questioning look on her face. It was as if she wasn't sure who he was. Then she smiled. Everything was back to normal now. Everything would be all right.

And it was. Jeanette saw to the details. She hustled Sean out of the house before calling the police. The story she concocted was perfect, how she'd gone to the library and come home to find her mother in the bathtub. How she'd pulled her from the water and tried artificial respiration, then called the police and the paramedics. How she'd calmly led them upstairs. The officers made a point of putting in their reports just how brave the young woman was.

So there was no question about what happened. With no father around, Jeanette inherited the house and her mother's insurance policy. She sold the house, moved in with an elderly couple and bided her time. She told Sean that stress had caused her to lose the baby, and he accepted it, just as she knew he would. When he signed a letter of intent with the university, she followed, paying for her tuition with what little money she had left.

Sean hadn't even suited up for his first practice before they were married.

Four years and three NCAA rushing records later, she was at his side when he signed a multi-million-dollar professional contract. Their future was made, the future that Jeanette had visualized from the beginning.

How could she have foreseen the injury? It happened during the third game of Sean's rookie season. The quick cut on astroturf, Sean's cleat catching a tear in the carpet just as a 250-pound, all-star linebacker hit him at the knees. The tackle almost tore his leg off. Four operations and six months of physical therapy made sure that he would again walk. But his career was over.

And, quickly enough, so was their marriage. Jeanette hadn't left Spokane just to end up stuck with a near-cripple on a fast track to nowhere. No, Sean might have had plans to return to school, get a teaching credential and coach high-school football, but he'd do it without Jeanette.

So she skipped. She cleaned out their account, leaving only what she couldn't cash in, and disappeared. She changed her name, lived in Europe awhile but eventually settled in a Mexican resort city on the Pacific. She lived well, keeping to herself and dodging the occasional investigator that she was sure had been sent by Sean.

But then the money ran out, and the good life ended.

Which was why she was back in Spokane. It was where Sean had returned. He had indeed gone back to work for his father. And, these five years later, his father now dead, Sean was doing well. He'd modernized the business, opened several branch locations. He'd even set up an Internet site.

He'd invested well, too. So well that he didn't have to work at all. He may have turned out to be a disappointment as a football player, but he'd become quite a successful businessman.

She'd called him that afternoon, using a phony name and title to get past his secretary. But he recognized her right away.

"Jeanette," he'd said. But then he went silent.

Until she told him that she was back. For keeps. That she was still his wife, that she still had feelings for him—"That never changed, you know that, baby," she'd said—and she wanted to see him.

Sean was still silent, and Jeanette was just about to get angry when he spoke.

"OK," he said. "Tonight. At eight. I take it you remember where I live."

She did, and she said as much. So the meeting was set.

And now Jeanette was ready to claim what was hers. She took one last look at herself in the mirror, then picked up her bag and left the motel room. She stowed the bag in the rental car's trunk, along with everything she owned in the world. Then she pulled out of the motel parking lot and headed for the South Hill.

Sumner Avenue was all but deserted on this cool fall night. Jeanette drove down the narrow street, piles of orange and yellow leaves covering both the asphalt and the wide expanse of lawns that fronted one mansion after the next. When she arrived at Sean's, she pulled up the driveway and around to the carriage house, just as he'd directed her. She parked in the dim light, and then she headed for the back door of the main residence.

She appraised the property as she walked. Things appeared to be well taken care of. This pleased her. She was particularly happy to see that Sean had apparently broken ground on what looked to be a swimming pool. A bulldozer sat near what would be the shallow end. Jeanette saw herself pool-side, drink in hand, the sun beating down, Sean waiting nearby.

The house was dark except for a glow that came, Jeanette knew, from the study. Many nights Jeanette and Sean had crept into that oak-lined sanctuary, Sean's father's sanctuary, and made love on the Persian carpet. Feeling a thousand-dollar carpet at her back had been almost as much a turn-on as feeling Sean inside her.

She rang the bell, waited a moment, then rang again. Jeanette could see her breath in the cool air. The whine of a car backing down a nearby driveway was the only sound that broke the silence. She was about to ring again when the door opened.

The kitchen light flicked on, and Sean was there. He hadn't changed much. A bit heavier, his hairline slightly higher, but unmistakably Sean. Still the athletic grace as he pushed open the heavy screen door. Still the easy charm as he smiled in recognition. Still the trusting attitude as he beckoned her inside.

Neither of them said anything. Yet as she brushed past him, not accidentally, it was clear that a current passed between them. As he closed the door and turned toward her, she turned back toward him. They suddenly were in each other's arms. Their embrace quickly turned into a kiss, one that Jeanette gave open-mouthed. She could feel his hardness. This is going to be easy, she thought.

It was Sean who pulled away.

"I'm sorry," he murmured. "I shouldn't be doing this."

"Why not?" Jeanette purred, again pulling close. "It's always been like this between us. No matter what else has happened, we've always had this."

"That's just it," Sean said, his voice hardening. "We've always had this but not a hell of a lot more." He pushed her away. "That much was clear when you left."

"Oh, baby," Jeanette said. But Sean ignored her. He turned away and limped down the hallway. Jeanette followed him, still trying to figure out the best way to play the scene. She stepped into the study just as Sean flopped into his father's leather chair. Jeanette stopped at the doorway. Something was different about the room. Then she noticed.

"Where's the carpet?" she said.

"I sold it," Sean said. "It didn't go with the new drapes. Besides, it brought back too many shitty memories."

Jeanette regarded the drapes and was barely able to mask her smirk. "Those look like something that Martha Stewart would recommend," she said. "Not that that's a bad thing."

"What do you want, Jeanette?" Sean said. "You didn't come here to talk about home redecoration."

Jeanette smiled again. She walked up to Sean, then crouched in front of him. She placed her hand on his knees. "No," she said, "that isn't why I came. I came because I still care about you, and I wanted to see if there was any chance for us."

"Any chance?" Sean scoffed. "Jeanette, I'll say it again. You left me. You took everything that wasn't nailed down and you disappeared. I spent what little I had left looking for you, figuring that you might have been kidnapped or something. But there was no note, no ransom demand. You were gone without a trace, and I was left with nothing. If it hadn't been for dad and...well, if it hadn't been for those who loved me, I don't know what I would have done."

"Oh, Sean, I'm so sorry," Jeanette said. "I didn't want to leave you, you have to know that."

"Then why, Jeanette?" Sean said. "Tell me why you left."

Jeanette stood up and walked to the window. Careful now, she told herself, just do it the way you practiced. She took a deep breath.

"Look, baby, I don't expect you to understand this, but I had to. Our whole life was based around you, around your career, your needs. There just wasn't any room for me to be me. I was stifled, suffocated. Our friends were your football friends. Our social engagements were like team meetings. We never even took a vacation until you...well, until you hurt yourself."

"I was just beginning my career," Sean said, a slight whine creeping into his voice. Jeanette had always hated that whine. "You knew that. I had to prove myself, then it was going to be easy street. Besides, you never seemed to complain. You seemed to be having a good enough time."

And she had been. Those parties had been what she'd been dreaming about since the first time she'd ever seen Sean run for a first down. There had been music, drink, ready blow, and even a clinch or two with that wide receiver that Sean had never found out about. No, the parties were exactly what she had wanted. The problem came when the parties stopped.

"I'm a good actor, Sean," she said. "I was trying to be a good wife to you."

Sean said nothing. It's working, Jeanette told herself. I truly am a good actress. She turned, and this time she dropped to her knees in front of him. Sean wore that simpering expression he always had when he was about to cave in to one of Jeanette's demands. She felt a thrill of power.

"And I still want to be a good wife to you," she said. She took his hands in hers, kissing his fingers. "I want us to be married again. I want us to start over."

Sean closed his eyes. He shook his head.

"I can't," he said.

"Sure you can," Jeanette said. "It'll be easy. You never tried to divorce me, I know that. And it wasn't just because you couldn't find me. You didn't do it because you still loved me."

At these words, Sean's eyes snapped open. Jeanette could see how the truth of what she'd said surprised him. This is too easy, she thought.

"Yeah, you still love me. And I still love you. And that's why this is so perfect. We're bonded, you and me. We belong together. We once had a dream and it ended, a long time before either of us wanted it to. Now we can have another. I know you've done well for yourself. But now that I'm back, it's time to take it easy. Oh, Sean, I've been around the world, and I've seen how great it is to travel in style. Your father left you a fortune, and you've made even more. We can live the way we always wanted. You know we can. We can have everything."

Sean shook his head again. "No," he said, "we can't."

"But why?" Jeanette said. "Give me just one reason why not."

It happened quicker than Jeanette could have imagined. Sean glanced over her head, and as she turned to see what he was looking at something flashed before her eyes. Then something was constricting her throat, and Sean was suddenly holding her wrists.

"Sean won't tell you, but I will," a voice hissed into her ear. "You can't get back together because I won't let you."

Jeanette wasn't prone to panic. No matter the situation, she'd always been able to handle herself. She'd walked through the toughest bars in Puerto Vallarta, confident in her ability to deal with whatever and whomever. But this was something different. She couldn't move, couldn't breathe, and worst of all she didn't know what was happening. She wanted to scream, but that was impossible. Whatever had been pulled around her neck was choking her. She struggled, but she was caught between Sean in front and someone—she had no idea who—in back. So she fought to regain her composure, to stay calm. There was a way out of this. All she had to do was keep her cool.

"You thought you were so smart, didn't you," the voice said. "Come marching back in here and manipulate Sean just the way you always have. Then, when he wasn't looking, you'd take off again with whatever you could grab."

It was a woman's voice, and Jeanette thought it sounded familiar. Whoever it was had pulled up closely against Jeanette, giving her no room to maneuver. She growled as she pulled the garrote even tighter. "But there was no way I was going to let that happen."

Jeanette gagged, but she raced through her alternatives. Couldn't outmuscle the two of them, so escape through force was out of the question. Couldn't expect to negotiate with his madwoman, whoever she was, so that wouldn't work either. She could just barely breathe, much less talk, so that just left Sean. She would have to work on Sean. And that meant using what she'd always depended on. Her body. She looked at Sean, her lips moving, her eyes filled with pleading.

"I know what you're thinking," the woman whispered. "I know everything about you. I know that you think Sean will weaken, that he'll let you loose. Maybe even do what you want, play house again. That's what you're thinking, isn't it?"

Jeanette's head pounded as she pulled herself closer to Sean. His grip was steady, his massive fingers evenly splayed around her wrists. He was still looking over her head.

"But you can just forget it," the woman said. "And let me tell you why. Haven't you wondered by now who I am?"

Jeanette pulled harder. The pressure on her throat hurt, and she was beginning to see spots at the corner of her vision. But Sean's fingers were just inches from her breasts. She was sure that once he felt her softness, he would hesitate, that he would look at her. And then she would be able to change his mind. But then she began to think about what this woman had asked her. Who, indeed, was she?

"You don't know, do you?" the woman said. She barked a short, bitter laugh. "Well, why should you? The last time you saw me we were in high school. I wore glasses, was flat-chested and ordinary, while you were Miss Hot Body. Yeah, I was the girl you took Sean away from."

Jeanette would have laughed had she been able. The geek! She thought she could win Sean back! Jeanette, conscious that she was close to passing out, pulled even harder.

"But I'm not that same girl now, you see," the geek said. Then again she laughed. "But I guess you don't see. You can't see me, and it must be killing you. Because you don't know, you can't know, whether I'm still flat-chested or whether I weigh three-hundred pounds. You don't know what you're up against, and this is just now beginning to scare you. Because you can't check out your competition."

A small nugget of doubt crept into Jeanette's consciousness, but she willed it away. Instead, she willed Sean to look at her. And, finally, he did.

"It wouldn't make any difference if you could, though," the geek said. "Because, as I said, I know you. I know there was no baby. That you pretended to do away with it. Did you know that Sean never suspected? I know what happened to your mother, too, and that Sean was slowly dying of guilt until I convinced him that it wasn't his fault. That you had planned the whole thing, that you would have ruined him to save yourself, and that you would have found some other way to kill her anyway."

Sean stared deeply into Jeanette's eyes, and through a red haze she could see him start to cry. He really did have beautiful eyes, she thought. She felt his knuckles brush the front of her blouse.

"And I know something else, too," the geek said. "I know what you don't, though you might suspect.

I know that I've loved Sean since I could remember. I know that I've never stopped loving him and believing that one day we would be married. I wasn't sure how it would come to be, because you were still out there some place, always a threat to return. But I just had faith that it would work."

With her last bit of strength, Jeanette arched her back, pushing her breasts onto Sean's knuckles, pleading with everything she had left for him to simply reach out and take them in hand, to reclaim them, and her, as his. But his expression never changed. Not in the slightest.

"And you did come back," the geek said, laughing. "And when you called Sean, he called me. And I was ready. And now you know what's going to happen? You're going to die. I'm going to kill you and bury you out where our new swimming pool is going to go. I had Sean burn that horrible carpet that you two fucked on because I couldn't stand even the thought of walking on it. But I'll tell you this. I am going to enjoy every minute of swimming laps in that pool, knowing that you're lying underneath it."

Jeanette would have screamed with rage. But then the geek jerked her neck back, and the world went black.

Death at Sunrise
By Colin Conway

The cell phone vibrated on the nightstand next to Shane McAfee's head. His eyes fluttered open. He lazily reached out and picked up the phone. The caller ID screen told him the department was calling.

He closed his eyes and opened the cell phone. "McAfee," he whispered.

"Shane? It's Laura. Where are you?"

He was silent for a moment before Laura continued.

"There's a suspicious death we need you to go out on."

"It's Saturday," Shane said.

"I know that, but you're next on the call list. The Captain wanted me to tell you you're flying solo on this. There's a double homicide out in Rockford so we're stretched thin."

"Damn."

"Since your call looks like a suicide he thought you could handle it on your own."

Shane reached over and caressed the naked hip

of the young woman lying next to him.

"Shane?"

Shane blinked a couple of times at the morning sunlight streaming in through the blinds. The room had a hazy glow to it. "What's the location?" he asked.

"The Sunrise Camp for Boys and Girls."

"It's a kid?"

"A teenager."

"Shit," he said and snapped the phone closed.

Shane rolled over and stared into the sleeping face of the woman next to him. Emily had recently celebrated her twenty-first birthday. He was closing in on his thirty-eighth. "Emily, wake up," he whispered.

Emily rolled on to her side, exposing her breasts. She touched Shane's chest and softly moaned. Her eyes were closed against the morning light.

"I need to go."

Emily's eyes slowly opened. "Why?"

"It's work."

She snaked her hand around Shane's waist and pulled herself to him. His body instinctively reacted. "Stay with me," Emily said with a playful smile.

Shane shook his head. "I can't. There's been a death."

"Yuck," she said and rolled over onto her stomach.

Shane slapped Emily's ass and stood up. "My sentiments exactly."

It took Shane almost thirty minutes of driving before he pulled into the dirt parking lot in front of several brown buildings at the Sunrise Camp for Boys and Girls located at the northeastern tip of Shelby Lake thirty miles north of Spokane. His clothes were the same ones he had worn in the office yesterday: a black polo shirt, a pair of blue jeans and a black pair of shoes. His .38 rested in his hip holster and his badge was attached to his belt.

Shane had visited the camp once before after a young camper went missing. They found the little boy an hour later, lost in the woods. Shane would have given a day's pay to be up there for the same reason.

When he turned the car off, the radio went silent.

"Nice car, McAfee."

Shane glanced over at the voice and saw Sergeant John Lee walking towards him. "Idiot," he muttered and climbed out of the car.

"Does that little toy help you pick up high school girls?" Lee asked with a snicker.

Shane ignored the comment. He'd been getting a lot of crap since he had started dating Emily. "Do you want to show me what you found?"

Lee motioned for Shane to follow and he headed toward a dirt path. The path was thin and disappeared into the nearby woods. A young deputy stood at the beginning of the path. Shane nodded at him as they walked by.

The two cops followed the path as it dropped down near the water line. On the left was a steep hillside speckled with smaller cabins. Each cabin had a set of wooden stairs that brought them back to the path. On the right was Shelby Lake.

Shane silently followed Lee until the Sergeant stopped and pointed at a small structure on the hill. "That's the victim's cabin."

"Is he up there?"

"No."

"Anybody ID him yet?"

"His name's Trevor Nash. Eighteen years old."

"I thought this was a camp for little kids."

"Is that why you came down here? Trying to find a new squeeze?"

Shane spun Lee around and stuck his finger in the Sergeant's face. "Get off my back."

Lee lifted his hands in mock surrender. "Relax, man. Banging that girl has given you a poor attitude."

Shane cocked his hand, ready to punch Lee in the mouth. The Sergeant scrambled back away from Shane and fell into the dirt. He clambered quickly to his feet, but stood his ground. They glared at each other, their hands balled into fists.

"You two assholes knock it off." Lieutenant Max Reisdorf hurried up the path toward them.

Lee pointed a finger at Shane. "He was going to deck me, Lieutenant."

Reisdorf stepped in between the two men. "John, go back up to the parking lot and wait for the coroner."

"But I didn't start this—"

"I don't care. You're up at the parking lot."

Shane kept his mouth shut as Sergeant Lee stormed off towards the camp's entrance. When he was out of sight, Shane turned back to the Lieutenant. "I'm sorry, Lieutenant, but Lee's riding me pretty hard."

"Stop riding the mayor's daughter, and he'll stop riding you."

Shane opened his mouth to protest, but the Lieutenant cut him off by pointing up to the cabin. "That's where the kid was staying."

"Yeah, Lee told me that. What he didn't say was why an eighteen-year-old kid is at summer camp."

"He's an advisor."

"An advisor? What's he do?"

"He advises. How the hell do I know what he does? He stayed up in that cabin. It's taped off and one of our own is up there sitting guard on it."

Shane looked around and suddenly realized how quiet the camp was. "Where is everybody?"

"All of the advisors and additional staff are sitting up in the cafeteria right now." Reisdorf look at his watch. "And to make matters worse, it's almost nine. The kids should be arriving in less than an hour."

"They're arriving today?"

Reisdorf nose crinkled and he nodded. "Yup."

"How many?"

"Two hundred."

"Shit."

"Tell me about it. I've been waiting the better part of an hour for you to bring your ass out here."

"I was delayed."

"I know what delayed you and I don't like it. Let's go."

The two men hurried down the path until it came to a clearing covered in dirt and sand. The clearing opened up to a view of the water. Morning sunlight shimmered on the lake.

The waterline was a couple of feet below the land's edge. On the far side of the clearing was a dock that jutted out into the water. The path that brought them to the clearing continued on the opposite side but disappeared into thicker foliage.

Reisdorf pointed up. "There he is."

Shane followed Reisdorf's finger then quickly stepped back. Hanging from a large tree was a young man in a dirty white t-shirt and khaki shorts. "Damn. Why isn't he cut down?"

"He's too high for us to get at."

"How did he get up there?"

"The rope swing starts off up there." Reisdforf pointed to a perch on the hillside. "The kids launch themselves over this clearing and out above the water."

"How do they get the rope back after someone's jumped?"

The Lieutenant pointed at the kid's foot. A smaller rope was tangled around his ankle. "They have a thinner rope tied to the main line. That's what they use to get the rope up to the next kid."

"Are we going to let him hang up there until his head finally pops off?"

"The coroner's on the way and we asked for several ladders to be brought out here."

Shane studied Travis Nash. He hung nine feet above the clearing floor. The rope was almost still, but the kid's body turned slightly in the morning breeze. If anyone climbed up onto the large branch to cut the rope, the kid would fall several feet before anyone would have the chance of catching him. Too much evidence would be destroyed.

Shane slowly walked up the hillside toward the rope swing's perch. The dirt along the area looked freshly disturbed. Shane glanced back at Travis' dirty t-shirt.

"Anyone take pictures of this trail?" There were random footprints in the rocky dirt, but nothing that seemed out of the ordinary.

"Yeah, we got some pictures already, but Forensics hasn't been through yet."

Shane nodded and continued walking up the path. He stopped at the jump-off point for the rope swing. The dirt looked compacted except for a few non-descript footprints. Twenty-five feet further up the hill and around the tree was another small perch with disturbed dirt.

"How about up here?"

Reisdorf looked up at Shane. "Yeah, we got pictures up there, too."

The small perch was closer to the tree and higher than the jump-off point. This perch would not allow someone to swing out over the clearing. Instead, if someone jumped at this point, it would be likely they would fall until the rope pulled taut.

"He went from up here where there was more slack in the rope."

"That's what I was thinking."

The tree stood at the edge of the perch and Travis Nash swung lightly in the breeze several feet from where Shane was standing. Shane leaned forward, his hand holding on to the tree for balance. He studied Travis as the body turned slowly in the wind. Shane saw blood on the back of his head.

"He was hit in the back of the head."

"What?"

Shane pushed away from the tree and stood upright. "The kid was hit in the back of the head with something. Have some of the guys fan out and look around for a weapon, maybe a big rock or something."

Reisdorf cocked his head to the side. "Everywhere you look there are rocks, bigger rocks and other heavy things. That's a bunch of possibilities."

Shane shrugged but kept his eyes on Travis Nash. "Then they need to get started."

Shane headed back toward the camp parking lot, wishing he was still in bed with Emily. He caught a whiff of her soap on his skin.

The morning sun brought some unseasonably warm heat with it. Beads of sweat formed on Shane's forehead as he continued along the path.

He stopped at the stairs leading up to Travis Nash's cabin. Shane was in good shape, but he was disappointed in himself for breathing so heavily after the walk up the path.

He grabbed the wooden handrail and pulled himself up the first step. Twenty-six steps later he walked onto the wooden sidewalk that led to Cabin number four. A young deputy leaned on a column supporting the porch roof. He immediately straightened up when he saw Shane.

"Sir?" he said.

"I'm Detective McAfee. Has anybody been in there?"

"I made a cursory sweep with Lieutenant Reisdorf before coming back out here."

"Anybody take pictures yet?"

"No, sir."

Shane thought about waiting for a deputy with a camera or the Forensics team but decided if he found anything he would record it later in his report. "I'm going in and take a look. Call for someone to come up here and snap some photos."

The deputy grabbed his shoulder microphone and called dispatch. Shane stepped by him and entered the cabin. Inside was a single large bay with ten bunk beds, five to each side of the room. The mattresses were bare and the floor recently swept. Against both walls and located between the second and third bunks were empty desks.

Shane slowly walked into the open room, his eyes sweeping top to bottom, left to right, searching for anything that could help him. He noticed the room smelled like Pine-Sol.

The empty camp would soon be filled with children, and the order and cleanliness of this moment would be lost for the summer.

Shane walked to the back of the cabin and found two smaller rooms. One was a bathroom with two stalls, two showers and two sinks. Across from the bathroom was the second room. A simple plaque hung on the door. It read *Advisor*.

The door was slightly ajar. Shane peeked through a crack between the door and the frame before slowly pushing the door open. He was careful not to touch the metal door knob.

The room contained a single bed covered with a bedspread and sheets. The top sheet was rolled over the edge of the bedspread. A single pillow rested at the top of the bed. In the corner of the room was a desk with a laptop computer. Shane checked the computer and found it turned off.

Near the head of the bed was a dresser. Shane pulled open each of the drawers by the edges and found underwear and socks in the top drawer, shorts and t-shirts in the second drawer; the bottom drawer contained a couple pairs of jeans and polo shirts. All of the clothing was neatly folded.

Shane glanced around the room again. The morning sunlight highlighted the floor. It was freshly swept.

He got on his hands and knees to look under the bed where he found a pair of flip-flops. He looked between the mattress and metal support wires, but found nothing. Shane pushed himself to his knees and leaned on the bed.

"Damn," he said and started to stand. His hand went to the pillow and flipped it over. Underneath was a folded piece of paper.

"Damn," Shane said again.

He unfolded the piece of paper and read the words on the sheet. Shane laid the paper on the bed and pulled out his notebook. He quickly copied the letter's content.

Shane refolded the paper and placed it under the pillow. After a final glance around the room, he went outside.

"Hey," he called to the young deputy. "Is the camera on the way?"

"Yes, sir. Forensics will take care of it when they do their sweep."

Shane pointed back at the cabin with his thumb. "Let them know there's a letter under the pillow on the Advisor's bed and that I didn't touch anything else."

The deputy nodded and Shane headed toward the stairs.

"What did the letter say?"

Shane stopped and glanced back at the deputy. "It said he killed himself."

Shane walked back up the path and contacted the deputy standing guard at the path's entrance.

"Hey, Marty, do me a favor and call Reisdorf. Ask him to meet me up here."

"Sure," Marty said and reached for his shoulder mike.

Shane walked into the large grassy area and lifted his face to the sun. It felt good and he smiled.

"Are you the detective?"

He blinked a couple of times at a skinny man in a blue polo shirt and khaki shorts. His shirt was neatly tucked and the khakis were recently ironed. His brown hair was short and combed precisely. The man stood roughly equal in height to Shane's six feet. He stuck his hand out and waited for Shane to take it.

"Yeah, I'm the detective," Shane said and shook his hand.

"I'm David Palmer, the camp's director."

"What can I do for you, Mr. Palmer?"

"I can't believe this is happening."

Shane nodded. "These things can be upsetting."

"Yes, yes, it most certainly is." Palmer turned around and pointed at the parking lot. "Any moment the buses are going to arrive with roughly two hundred children. I need to know what to do."

"Turn them around and send them home," Shane said.

Palmer smiled and shook his head. "I can't do that."

"Why?"

"Because the Sunrise Camp provides services for various churches and organizations. The groups coming for this session are from churches as far away as Walla Walla and Moses Lake. Some are from Spokane, but most are from outlying cities. Their ride here is almost three hours."

Shane nodded. "I understand your problem, David, but I can't have the kids running around while we complete our investigation. When the buses arrive, have them park in the lot. Don't let the kids come into the camp until I tell you. Okay?"

"What about food and water?"

"I'll do what I can to clear some advisors so they can help with that."

"Okay," Palmer said with a sigh of resignation.

"Now, let me ask you a couple questions."

Palmer's eyes focused on the detective.

"Who called 911 to report the kid's death?"

"I did—from my office. Most cell phones won't work out here."

Shane pulled his cell phone from its case. The screen showed no service

"How did you find the kid's body?"

Palmer shook his head. "I didn't find the body. Mark Brown did."

"Who's Mark Brown?"

"He's an advisor here. He stays in cabin number three."

"So, Mark Brown found Travis Nash hanging in the tree and came running to you?"

"That's what he told me. We immediately called the police."

"Did you go down and see the body?"

"Yes, I did. Afterwards. It's very sad."

Shane nodded in agreement. "Where is Mark Brown right now?"

"He and the rest of the staff are in the cafeteria." Palmer pointed at a long brown building.

Behind the cafeteria was the administration building. Shane had noticed it on the way in. The building to the east was a small brown affair. Behind it were two small buildings. Shane pointed at both of them. "What's in those buildings?"

"The furthest one is the maintenance shed. The closer one is the nurse's office."

"Are there computers in any of the buildings?"

"Yes, there's a computer in the nurse's station, one in my office in the admin building, and one in the lounge of the cafeteria building."

"Can the advisors use any of those?"

Palmer shook his head. "Only one. The one in the admin building is used only by me. The nurse's station is locked and for the nurse only. The advisors can only use the computer in the cafeteria building."

Shane rubbed his chin and felt a day's worth of stubble. "Do me a favor and ask Mark to come out and talk with me. No one except you is allowed to leave the cafeteria at this time. Understood?"

"Yes, sir," Palmer said and hurried off to the cafeteria.

Shane pulled out his notebook and made a few entries.

Lieutenant Reisdorf walked up to Shane, a sheen of sweat on his forehead. "You sent for me?" Reisdorf said, the irritation clear in his voice.

"I checked out the kid's cabin already," Shane said and tucked the notebook back into his pocket. "I found a letter under his pillow."

"What'd it say?"

Shane studied the cafeteria building as he spoke. "It said Travis was sorry for touching several little boys. He couldn't take the guilt and decided to kill himself."

"I guess that settles it."

Shane's looked at Reisdorf. "How do you figure?"

"The kid left a suicide note."

"What about the blood on the back of his head?"

"He probably cracked it against the tree after he jumped and swung around bit."

Shane shrugged. "That's a theory, but there's still the problem with the note."

Reisdorf stepped in front of Shane and put his hands on his hips. "And what problem is that exactly?"

"The suicide note was done on a computer printer."

"So?"

"There's no printer in Travis Nash's room."

Reisdorf crossed his arms over his chest. "Mmmm."

"That's what I thought," Shane said. "I'm going to need a couple things."

"Tell me it doesn't involve manpower. I'm stretched too thin as it is."

"I need someone to secure the computer in the cafeteria."

"Shit," Reisdorf muttered. "Where am I going to get more people?"

Shane shrugged. "You'll figure it out. That's why you're the Lieutenant."

"Anything else?"

"I need someone to check out all the cabins to see if anyone has a computer and printer inside."

"That'll take some time."

"I've got plenty of time." Shane pointed to the buses pulling into the parking lot. "But those kids are going to get pretty restless sitting in those sardine cans."

Mark Brown was a good looking kid. His angular features, bushy brows and dark eyes were the type young girls would fawn over. He had the athletic build of a football player: tall, muscular and lean. He wore a clean white t-shirt that said *Sunrise Camp* and a pair of clean khaki shorts. On his feet were a pair of flip-flops.

His eyes were nervous, though, as he approached Shane. "Mr. Palmer said you asked for me."

Shane waved for Mark to follow him, and the two walked over to a picnic table in the grassy area, out of sight from the buses.

"Grab a seat."

Mark slowly sat down, his eyes never leaving the detective.

Shane pulled out his notebook and laid it on the table in front of him. "You found Travis this morning?"

Mark nodded.

"And then you reported it immediately to the camp director?"

"Yeah, that's exactly what I did."

"Tell me how you found Travis."

"I was heading toward the cafeteria to get breakfast and I saw him hanging there."

"What time was this?"

"About eight."

Shane made a quick entry in his notebook. "How well did you know Travis?"

"We've worked at the camp for the past couple of years. He worked with the maintenance crew, and I worked in the cafeteria. Those were our junior and senior years of high school. We're college freshmen now, so we're finally advisors."

"What college do you guys go to?"

"I go to Eastern. Travis goes to Gonzaga."

"Were you two close?"

Mark shook his head.

"Why not?"

"I think he's gay, so I really don't want to be around him."

"Is that why you hit him this morning?"

Mark's eyes widened. "What?"

"You didn't like him because he's a fag so you hit him."

"No," Mark said. His mouth hung open in astonishment.

"Did he make a pass at you? That's probably why you hit him, right?"

"I didn't hit him at all!" Mark's voice rose in panic.

"I'm not sure I can believe that."

"Why?"

"You've already lied to me about how you found him, so now I think you're lying about killing him."

"He committed suicide."

"And you lied to me."

"How?"

"You're in cabin number three, and Travis stayed in cabin number four. Cabin number six sits right next to the clearing where Travis' body was found. If you walked to the cafeteria from your cabin you would never have passed Travis' cabin or his body hanging from the tree."

Mark lowered his head, and his tongue darted across his lips.

"At this point, you probably want to start telling the truth."

Mark looked up at Shane. He glanced over his shoulder and then leaned in toward the detective. "If I tell you something, do you promise to keep it confidential?"

"No," Shane said and put his elbows on the table.

Mark thought for a moment before speaking. "If anyone finds out about this, I'll get kicked out of camp and never allowed to work the summers again."

Shane's face remained passive.

"I spent the night with Mindy Monahan."

"Where does Mindy stay?"

"Cabin nine."

Shane rubbed his chin and watched the kid.

"It's forbidden for staff to have sexual relationships with another staff member. Anyone found doing it would be immediately excused from the camp. This is a great summer gig and I don't want to lose it."

Shane thought about telling the kid he should control his urges, but the image of Emily popped into his mind. The entire department had been giving him a hard time about controlling his own desires.

"Mindy can vouch for this?"

"Do you have to ask her?"

"I've got to rule you out as a suspect."

Mark dropped his head.

Shane stood up and said, "Follow me."

They walked over to the parking lot and Shane waved over Sergeant Lee. "John, have this kid sit in your car for a few minutes."

Lee grabbed Mark by the elbow. He escorted the kid to his patrol car and put him in the back seat. When he returned to Shane, Lee looked clearly put out. "I sure as hell hope you're not going to interview each kid one by one. There's got to be twenty-five of them in the cafeteria and there are five bus loads of brats waiting to start their camp."

"I'm working it as fast as I can."

Shane was met by an elderly man in a brown and green uniform, similar to those the deputies were wearing. He was a volunteer Shane had seen around before but had never learned his name. "The Lieutenant said you needed someone to watch over a computer."

Shane nodded and they headed towards the cafeteria.

Immediately inside the cafeteria building was a small lounge. Several couches and chairs filled the room. In the corner sat a large wooden desk with a computer and printer. On the opposite side of the room from where they were standing was the door to the cafeteria.

Shane pointed at the computer. "Don't let anyone near that desk or computer."

The old man nodded, "Yes, sir."

Shane headed into the cafeteria. Seated in the spacious room were about twenty-five teenagers and a few adults. Each of them had on the white Sunrise t-shirt and khaki shorts that seemed to be the camp uniform. When the detective stepped into the room, every head turned his way.

"Can I speak to Mindy Monahan?"

A young brunette raised her hand and slowly stood. She was a thin girl but properly proportioned. She got up and headed his direction as he walked back out to the picnic table where he had spoken with Mark. As Mindy walked toward him, she held her arms tightly around her stomach. Embarrassment was evident on her face.

Mindy sat at the table but kept her arms crossed over her body.

"Do you know why I called you out?"

She shook her head.

"Someone killed Travis, and I need to know who did it."

"But I thought he hung himself."

"That's not how it went down."

"Well, how did it happen?"

He shrugged. "I'm still working that out, but you need to tell me where you were last night and this morning."

"In my cabin."

"Alone?"

Mindy swallowed hard before nodding.

"Are you sure?"

She nodded again.

"Why do I get the feeling you're lying?"

Tears welled in her eyes.

"Did someone spend the night with you?"

"Yes."

"Who?"

"Mark."

Shane drummed his fingers on the table. "If I report this to Mr. Palmer, you both will be kicked out of the camp, right?"

Her head bobbed as tears flowed down her cheeks.

"Do you know of anyone who would want to hurt Travis?"

Mindy shook her head. "No."

"Did you see anyone using the computer in the cafeteria this morning?"

She wiped the tears from her face with the back of her hand. "No."

"Did you like Travis?"

Mindy shrugged. "I guess. He wasn't my favorite guy, but I didn't hate him."

"Did Travis have any friends?"

"Sure. His best friend would probably be Tom Baker."

"Tom?"

"Yeah. They seemed to hang out a lot."

Shane stood up. "Stay here," he said and headed back toward the parking lot and Sergeant Lee. A green Ford pick-up with three ladders in the back pulled into the parking lot, followed by a white van with the star-shaped logo of the Spokane County Sheriff's Office on its side. Forensics had finally arrived.

Lee met Shane, and both men watched the Forensics team unload their equipment.

"Sarge, you can use the girl and the kid in your car to bring snacks and water to the kids on the buses."

Lee's eyes narrowed. "Now you're telling me how to do my job?"

Shane shook his head. "No, I'm just telling you that I did mine and I'm letting those two walk right now. I thought they could be of some help to you."

Lee sniffed once. "Fine," he said and walked off to the Forensics team.

Shane headed back to the cafeteria and called out Tom Baker.

"You're a friend of Travis Nash?"

"Is it true what they've been saying?"

"What's that?"

"That Travis is dead?"

Shane nodded. "Yeah."

"I can't believe it."

Tom Baker was an awkward looking kid with long floppy hair and a gait that reminded Shane of an old horse. When he sat at the table, he looked like he was ready to pee his pants.

"Did he ever say anything to you about being depressed or wanting to hurt himself?"

Tom shook his head. "No. Travis was a pretty happy guy. He never complained about much and seemed to be happy working up here for the summer."

Shane leaned on the table. "Was Travis gay?"

Tom glanced over his shoulder and then back to the detective. "Why does that matter?"

The detective shrugged. "I'm not sure if it does."

Tom rubbed his face and then ran his fingers through his hair. "He wasn't gay."

"How can you be sure?"

Tom stared at Shane until the detective figured it out.

"You're gay."

"I won't admit it to you because I don't want to lose this job. Being a camp advisor is good money for hanging out in the sun for a few months."

"Did Travis have any enemies?"

"Not really. I'm sure there were people who didn't like him. But I don't think there was anyone who wanted him dead."

"What cabin do you live in?"

"Number one."

"Okay, Tom. Report to the Sergeant over there," Shane said and pointed to Lee. "He's going to have you get the kids some food and water."

Tom stood up and walked away.

Shane pulled out his notebook and plopped it onto the picnic table. He made some quick notes about Tom and then stared at his scribblings from earlier in the day.

He flipped a couple of pages back and reread his copy of the note he found under Travis Nash's pillow.

> *I am sorry for the things I've done. I can never tell you how much hurt I've caused to others because of my own perversion. In the past, I've touched boys and for that I'm deeply sorry. I can never be forgiven.*
> *- Travis*

Shane rubbed his chin and continued studying the words.

"Detective McAfee?"

He turned at the sound of his name to see a small woman with gray frizzy hair approaching. Shane recognized her immediately. County Commissioner Janet Carlson. Sergeant Lee was a foot behind her with an ugly grin on his face.

"Are you Detective McAfee?"

"Yes, ma'am."

"I'm deeply concerned at what is going on here."

"Me, too."

"Those children on the buses are not prisoners."

"I agree. Is your child on one of the buses?"

"No, but I *am* worried about those children."

"I'm concerned about them as well."

"I don't see how. You're making them stay on those buses."

Shane sighed. He was wasting time with a commissioner who served no purpose in a homicide investigation. "A murder happened here this morning, and I'd like to catch the killer before we let a group of children in."

The Commissioner stammered, "Murder? What murder? I thought it was a suicide."

"It's not."

Carlson pointed a manicured finger at Shane. "I want to know everything that led you to that conclusion."

"Ma'am, you're slowing down my investigation."

"It looks like you're doing nothing but sitting here."

"That's because I'm talking to you."

Janet Carlson's face pinched. "Detective, you're a liability to this department because of your personal life. You should thank your lucky stars you're even handling this case."

Shane shrugged. "Ma'am, if you want me off this case, the Lieutenant is down that path over there."

Carlson's cheeks turned red before she spun around and bumped into the grinning Sergeant. "Where is the Lieutenant?"

Lee bowed slightly. "It'd be my pleasure to show you the way."

The two of them hurried away from Shane.

Shane walked around the cafeteria to the administration building. He pulled open the screen door. It creaked loudly before banging behind him as he entered.

Before him a long counter provided a barrier between the visitors and administrators. David Palmer emerged from a rear office and walked up to the counter. "Detective?"

"Do you have files on all of the advisors?"

"Sort of. All of the staff, including the cooks and maintenance folks, must pass a background check. I've got the applications they filled out prior to starting this summer. No one has a file, though."

"Can I see the applications?"

"Sure," Palmer said and disappeared into his office. A moment later he returned and handed the detective a stack of applications.

Shane took the papers and flipped slowly through them. "Can I take these with me?"

Palmer shrugged. "I guess so. I'm not sure if there are any privacy laws I'm breaking though."

Shane ignored his concern and walked back to the cafeteria building. The senior volunteer was sitting on a folding chair near the computer.

"Anybody come by to use the computer?"

The old man shook his head. "No, sir."

Shane sat down at the computer. He pressed the power button and the machine whirred to life. A few moments later the monitor lit up and told Shane the computer had been improperly shut down. The computer ran a diagnostic check before flipping over to the familiar Windows screen.

Shane went to the Start menu and opened up the only word processor on the machine: Microsoft Word. It was the same program he used at the department to write his reports. When the program opened a side bar popped up and said that there was a recovered document that he could view.

A click on the side bar opened up the document. There on the monitor was the letter Shane had found under Travis Nash's pillow. He stared at the document for a moment.

"Find what you're looking for?" the old man asked.

"Yeah."

Shane moved the pointer up to the File menu and selected Properties from the available choices. The document's specifics popped up on the screen and showed it had been created at 7:56 that morning.

Shane made an entry into his notebook before turning to the volunteer. "This is part of the crime scene now. No one touches the computer except Forensics."

The old man nodded, grateful his efforts were important.

Shane hurried outside and pulled his cell phone from its holder. Still no service. In his left hand, he carried the applications for the staff. He headed toward the parking lot and saw a large crowd of children surrounding the buses. They appeared restless and anxious to get inside the camp.

Shane walked over to the Sergeant's car and climbed in. There on the Mobile Data Computer was all of the call information; including who called it in and where the call was from. In the upper right-hand corner, Shane found the time that 911 reported the call came in: 8:02 a.m..

The letter was created on the computer six minutes before the hanging was reported. There was no way Travis Nash could have returned to his cabin, put the letter under his pillow and then hung himself.

Shane now knew without a doubt Travis Nash was murdered and he could prove it. What he couldn't prove was who did it.

Possibilities ran through his mind as he jogged down the path. At the clearing, Lieutenant Reisdorf, Sergeant Lee and County Commissioner Carlson stood together. Their attention was focused entirely on Travis Nash as four forensic technicians prepared to cut his body down from the tree. Three ladders were set up in a triangle formation and a technician was at the top of each ladder. The technicians had attached a harness to Travis. A rope dangled from the other branch. A deputy on the ground held the loose rope and prepared for the weight of the body to be transferred to him.

Perched on the branch of the tree, a female technician carefully sawed the rope back and forth until it snapped free. The deputy immediately held tight to the rope and the body of Travis Nash was carefully guided to the ground by the three technicians.

Commissioner Carlson's face was white. "It's a shame for a boy to take his own life."

Shane coughed once. "It wasn't a suicide."

Lieutenant Reisdorf reached out, grabbed Shane by the arm, and escorted him away from the Commissioner. "What are you doing?"

"My job."

"No, I mean pissing off the Commissioner. She came down here with her panties in a bunch, wanting me to kick you off the case and suspend you."

"For what?"

"For being Shane McAfee."

"She's mad at me for my personal life. I can't help that."

"Shane, pull your head out of your ass."

"I'm trying."

Reisdorf spat on the ground next to him. "Fuck," he muttered. "Now I'm spitting at a crime scene. You're driving me nuts."

Shane caught the Commissioner watching them with alert eyes.

"Why is she here?" Shane asked.

"What do you mean?"

"She told me she didn't have a kid on one of those buses, so why is she here?"

"This is going to be a high-profile case. She probably wants the exposure when the camera crews show up."

"Have you ever had a commissioner out at a crime scene?"

"No, not really."

"Then why is she here?"

The Commissioner turned and headed up the path with Sergeant Lee at her side.

"What are those?" Reisdorf asked and pointed at the papers in Shane's hand.

"Huh? Oh, all of the staff here—their applications."

Reisdorf left to look at the body. Shane thumbed through the names of each advisor. There wasn't a single Carlson in the bunch. He flipped the stack over. On the back side of each paper was the emergency contact information for each advisor.

Shane slowly flipped through the papers backwards. Each advisor had to list two people in case an emergency occurred. About two-thirds of the way through the stack, Shane found what he was looking for. Janet Carlson was the emergency contact for Peter Reynolds. Relation to advisor: mother.

Shane pulled out Peter's form and skimmed through the information. For the last three years he had been a cafeteria team member for the camp. Before that, when he was in junior high school, he was an attendee at the camp. This year he would be an advisor.

Shane walked up the path and continued until he got to the administration building. The screen door squeaked to announce his presence, and David Palmer came out of his office again.

"I've been on the phone all morning trying to do damage control. You can't believe how fast word is traveling right now."

Shane held up Peter Reynolds' application. "Do you know this kid?"

Palmer nodded. "Sure. Good kid. He's kind of shy, but a hard worker nonetheless."

"Did he come in and use the phone this morning?"

"Not that I know of, but I wasn't in my office all morning."

"Do you normally leave it unlocked?"

"Sure. Who out here is going to steal something?"

"Did Peter know Travis?"

"Everybody knows everybody."

"I mean, did they know each other prior to this year?"

"Sure. They've both been at the camp for several years." David looked past Shane and through a window overlooking the parking lot. "Speak of the devil."

Shane turned around and saw Commissioner Carlson walking quickly towards a black Volkswagen Jetta. At her side was a younger man. "Is that...?"

"Peter Reynolds," Palmer said.

Shane dropped the papers on the counter and ran out of the office. The screen door banged loudly behind him.

Janet Carlson and Peter Reynolds glanced back at the noise.

"Stop!" Shane yelled.

"Get in the car, Peter!" Janet barked at her son.

Peter opened the car door and sat down.

Shane sprinted across the parking lot, his vision tunneled on the Commissioner and her son. He didn't see Sergeant Lee climb out of his patrol car and race toward him. Shane was almost to the Volkswagen when Lee reached out and grabbed his arm. Shane spun and crashed to the ground. Pieces of gravel tore into his elbows and arms. He scrambled back to his feet, ready to launch at the Sergeant.

The Commissioner climbed into her car and shut the door.

"What the hell do you think you're doing?" Shane yelled at Lee.

"You were going to attack a commissioner."

The two officers were standing behind the Commissioner's car, blocking it from backing out.

Shane pointed at the car. "She's leaving with her kid. That's interfering with an investigation."

Lee shook his head. "He didn't do anything. She just wants him out of here."

"How do you know he wasn't involved?"

"I asked him," the Sergeant said, crossing his arms over his chest.

"You talked to the kid?"

"Yeah, and he said he didn't see anything or do anything."

"Then why in the hell is she rushing him out of here?"

Lee shrugged but kept his arms crossed. "She wants to take him home."

Shane threw his arms up in the air. "No, shit, she wants to take him home!"

"I don't see the problem here."

"The problem is, he had to have called her this morning after the body was found. Otherwise, how else would she know to rush out here?"

Lee looked at the boy in the car.

"I still believe he didn't do it."

Shane pointed at the car. "Get the kid out of the car so I can talk to him."

"I'm a Sergeant in the department and you better show me some respect."

"If the Lieutenant finds out about you screwing this up...." Shane's voice trailed off.

Lee glared at Shane for a moment before dropping his arms and walking to the driver's door. He tapped on the glass, and Janet Carlson lowered the window. "I'm sorry, Commissioner, but I'm going to need Peter to step out and talk with Detective McAfee."

Janet opened her car door and stepped out. "I'm not letting my son talk to that misogynistic bastard. You already asked Peter your questions, and you said you believed him."

Lee bowed his head slightly. "It's not my investigation, ma'am."

"Who is the Sergeant here?"

"It doesn't matter," Lee said, his voice lowered and hushed.

"Call the Sheriff down here. I want to talk with him."

"Yes, ma'am."

"Commissioner," Shane said and stepped over to her. "Did your son play any role in the murder of Travis Nash?"

"No, of course not."

"Then let me talk to him."

Janet Carlson's face reddened, and her jaw muscles tightened, but she said nothing.

"Ma'am," Shane said, "We can still have the Sheriff come down here, but I don't think we should delay this any longer. We've got all of those kids waiting for camp to start."

Carlson looked toward the buses and the children. Shane imagined her counting the voting parents in her mind. "Peter stands by me when you ask your questions."

"That's fine," Shane said.

Janet Carlson bent down to the car. "Peter, please come out and talk with the detective."

Peter climbed out and stared at Shane. He stood about five-foot-eight with a bad case of acne. Peter glanced at the camp buildings. When he looked back, his eyes squinted.

Shane moved towards Peter, and the young man took a step back.

"Hey!" Shane said as the kid turned and ran. Shane tore after him.

"Peter!" Janet Carlson screamed.

"Stop!" Shane yelled.

Peter had the advantage of youth and quickness on his side, but Shane's stride was longer, and every few steps he gained a little distance. They raced to the end of the administration building before Peter pulled up, easing into a trot.

Shane tackled him and they rolled down the slight hill past the edge of the administration building and into a small clearing near the maintenance shed.

Peter struggled against Shane's grasp as the detective tried to put a pair of handcuffs on his wrists. "I didn't do it," Peter blurted.

Shane clicked the handcuffs into place and rolled the young man on to his back. "Then why'd you run?"

"I didn't know if they could see us."

"Who is *they*?"

Lee sprinted up to Shane. "You okay?"

"Yeah," Shane said.

"I was talking to the kid."

Shane looked back at Lee to comment, but the Sergeant had already grabbed his shoulder mike. "We got the kid. Everyone return to their positions."

Shane turned his attention back to Peter. "Who are you worried about seeing us?"

Peter jerked his head toward the maintenance shed.

Shane looked at the shed. "Is someone in there?"

"I dunno," Peter said. "But those are the guys you should start talking to."

Shane stood up, his eyes fixed on the shed. "Watch him," he said to Lee and headed toward the small building. Shane slowly pulled his gun out of its holster and let it hang by his leg.

The maintenance shed was about twenty feet by thirty feet. The sides were painted barn red and the metal roof was painted white. A padlock on the front door stopped Shane from getting in. He tugged on it a couple of times, hoping it would pop open. When it didn't, he walked around the shed and found there were no windows to peek through. From the corner of the roof, a small wind chime hung and tinkled lightly in the breeze.

Next to the building was a gravel area with a sign that read, *Maintenance Crew parking only*. In the middle of the gravel was a shiny white van with *Sunrise Camp for Boys and Girls* printed on it.

Shane studied the building a minute more before walking back to Peter. He slipped his gun back into its holster as he walked. Janet Carlson ran up to her son and stood in front of him, blocking Shane. "How dare you hurt my child!"

"Get out of the way," Shane said and reached past her toward Peter.

Carlson slapped her hand across Shane's arm.

The detective immediately jerked his hand back. He stepped close into the Commissioner. "If I wanted I could arrest you right now for assault of an officer. Either let me finish with your son, or I'll arrest you."

Sergeant Lee carefully reached out for the Commissioner. "Excuse me, ma'am. You need to let the detective finish talking with your son."

Carlson let herself be pulled away, but she kept her eyes squarely on Shane.

The detective reached down and lifted Peter to his feet. "What's with the maintenance shed?"

Peter looked around, his voice hushed. "There are two types of kids who do maintenance work at the camp. There are those who are doing it until they get to be an advisor. Those kids always get the grass mowing and landscaping jobs. Then there are those kids who connect with Albert, the maintenance supervisor, and those kids turn strange."

"Strange? What do you mean?"

"They don't hang out with the rest of us anymore. They do their job and that's it. Sometimes, during the summer, they come and go as they please for days at a time during a camp session. Normal advisors can't do that."

Shane remembered Nash's file. "Travis used to work on the crew."

Peter nodded. "Yeah, but he wasn't one of the strange ones."

"Why wouldn't you tell me this in the parking lot?"

"Travis and I talked last night after dinner. He thought he saw something but wouldn't tell me what it was. He didn't want to freak me out if it was nothing."

"Did he hint at what it was?"

"Travis said it dealt with Albert, and now he's dead. I don't know what's going on, but I don't want to be next."

"Who's on the maintenance crew?"

Peter gave him a list of names, explaining who worked the grounds and who was part of Albert's special crew. When he was done, Shane released Peter to his mother and went back to work. As the detective walked away, he could hear the Commissioner filing a complaint with Sergeant Lee.

The screen door to the administration building squawked as Shane yanked it open. When he stepped inside, he heard David Palmer say, "I gotta go." A moment later the camp director stepped into the front office.

Shane walked past the director and into his office.

Palmer protested. "Detective? Detective!"

Shane sat down on a wooden chair in front of the director's desk. Palmer slowly walked around and sat in his own chair. Shane noted the walkie-talkie that had been placed on top of a stack of papers in the middle of the desk.

"Detective, are you all right?"

Shane ran his fingers through his hair. "Who is Albert?"

David Palmer tilted his head. "What?"

"Albert? Who is he?"

"He's responsible for the maintenance of the campgrounds."

"Is he here all year round?"

"Yes."

"Does anyone else stay here all year long?"

"No one."

"What about you?"

"Besides me," Palmer said, his voice small.

"Only you and Albert are here all year long?"

Palmer nodded.

Shane studied the black telephone on Palmer's desk. "Who were you talking to when I walked in?"

"Who was I talking to?"

Shane smiled, knowing the camp director was stalling. He leaned forward in his chair. "Yeah, who were you talking to on the phone?"

"A concerned parent."

"Which one?"

"Uh, Ruth Anderson. Chuckie's mother."

Shane nodded. "Can I use the phone for a second?"

Palmer smiled and said, "Yes, of course."

Shane slid the phone over and lifted the receiver. It was cool in his hand. Shane's finger hovered above the redial button for a moment before he hung up the phone.

"You weren't on the phone, were you?"

"What?"

Shane stood up and grabbed the walkie-talkie. It was warm in his grip. "This is the first walkie-talkie I've seen since getting here. One unit by itself is worthless. It takes two to make a conversation. Who's on the other walkie-talkie?"

Palmer's face went slack, and he stared into Shane's eyes. Finally, he muttered "I didn't kill Travis."

"Who has the other unit?"

"Albert," David said.

"Albert who?"

"Albert Martin."

Shane clicked his tongue against his teeth. "Where can I find Albert?"

"I can't tell you."

Shane jumped to his feet. "Where is Albert?

Palmer shook his head and closed his eyes.

Shane's voice rose in anger. "Did Albert kill Travis?"

Palmer continued to shake his head.

"Did Albert kill Travis?" Shane demanded.

Palmer opened his eyes as tears streamed down his face. His mouth fell open but no answer came.

Shane slapped the desk. "Damn it, Palmer!" He yelled. "Did Albert kill Travis?"

"Yes," Palmer said, "Oh, God, yes."

Shane set the walkie-talkie back on the desk. It crackled to life. "I'm going to kill you, David," a low, menacing voice said.

Palmer's eyes widened. "You...had...the radio on."

Shane leaned over the desk. "Now tell me where Albert Martin is hiding before he gets to you."

Palmer wiped the tears from his face with the back of his hand. "There's a storage shed near cabin number eleven. He's in there."

Shane grabbed the walkie-talkie and ran out of the administration building, the door slamming closed behind him.

Shane sprinted to Sergeant Lee, who was standing near his patrol car. A dirty smile was on his face. "The Commissioner is going to have your balls."

"Shut up," Shane blurted, "and get on the radio."

"Watch yourself."

"Get on the fuckin' radio and tell some deputies to get to the storage shed near cabin number eleven. Nash's killer is hiding out there. His name's Albert Martin, and he's the maintenance supervisor. Also, go to the Admin building and watch Palmer. He's part of this."

Lee straightened up as he took in the gravity of Shane's words. The detective turned and sprinted toward the path, the walkie-talkie in his hand. His feet propelled him along the thin, twisting path. Step after step, his heart pounded harder.

Shane's right foot landed awkwardly on a rock and his ankle twisted, sending him to the ground. He dropped the walkie-talkie as he fell to catch himself. The skin on his hands, already torn up from the fall in the gravel, ripped open further. He grabbed the radio, scrambled to his feet and continued up the path, his ankle now screaming with pain.

He raced past the clearing and the Forensic team as they were bagging Nash's body. Lieutenant Reisdorf stared dumbfounded, as Shane sprinted by. All Shane heard was the Lieutenant say, "What the —"

At cabin eleven, Shane climbed up the steps, two at a time. When he reached the cabin he found three deputies, sweat on their faces and their guns drawn. "Behind the cabin," Shane said, trying his best to control his breathing. "The storage unit."

Deputy Ron Wolfe shook his head. "There ain't no storage unit here."

Shane took the words in and sprinted behind the cabin. He spun around looking for anything resembling a man-made structure. There was nothing. Deputy Wolfe came around the building and stood next to him.

"Shit," the detective said.

"You want us to fan out and look deeper into the woods?"

Shane shook his head. "The camp director would know exactly where a storage unit was. He sent me on a wild goose chase. Contact Sergeant Lee and have him hold on to David Palmer until I get back there."

Shane bent over and put his hands on his knees, trying to regulate his breathing. He listened as Wolfe tried to reach Sergeant Lee on the police radio. On the third try, Wolfe looked over at Shane. "He's not answering."

"Get someone there now," Shane said. The detective ran to the path, his legs straining as he raced, his right ankle tightening up. Sweat burned his eyes as he darted past the clearing where the Lieutenant was watching over the Forensic team.

His stomach ached as he climbed toward the entrance to the administration building. A yank of the screen door and he was inside. Lying behind the counter was Sergeant John Lee. He moaned as he struggled to his feet.

Shane hopped over him and into the office of the camp director. It was empty. Shane went back to the Sergeant. "What happened?"

"I don't know. I turned my back on Palmer for a second and then I was on the floor."

Shane leaned against the counter. He keyed the microphone on the walkie-talkie he had taken from Palmer and lifted it to his mouth. "Albert, where are you?'

There was no answer.

"Albert, this is Detective McAfee. I need to talk with you."

The radio was silent.

"David, if you are with Albert, you're just as guilty of killing Travis."

The radio crackled to life. A soft noise tinkled before a voice said, "Go to Hell."

The tinkling noise was familiar and Shane struggled to place it. He stepped outside and looked around. The kids from the buses were milling about in the parking lot near the opening to the camp. He could hear them talking excitedly among themselves and many were staring at him. Mark Brown and Mindy Monahan moved toward him, concern showing on their faces.

An engine fired up, and Shane looked over his shoulder, down the length of the Admin building. Then he remembered the tinkling sound from the wind chime hanging at the maintenance shed.

The nose of the maintenance van turned the corner and pointed right at him. The berm was to his right. The Admin building and the cafeteria were to his left. The only way out for the van was through Shane and into the parking lot which was now inhabited by two hundred children.

Shane turned toward the kids. "Get back!" he screamed at Mark and Mindy. "Get them back!"

Shane spun back around as the van lurched forward, its engine roaring. In a single motion the detective dropped the radio and drew his Smith &

Wesson. He squeezed the trigger repeatedly, the gun bouncing in his hand. The children behind him screamed wildly.

The van swerved several times before colliding with the Admin building, tearing off chunks of wooden siding. Shane jumped out of the way, his feet and hands propelling him up the side of the berm.

The van freed itself from the building but swung wildly to the left and up the berm. It bottomed out and suddenly stopped a few feet in front of Shane.

The detective stood up and moved toward the van, his gun leading the way. David Palmer was in the passenger seat, a deflating air bag in front of him. Shane pulled open the door and reached out to press two fingers against Palmer's neck. He was breathing, but unconscious.

Shane stepped up the berm and around the front of the van to see Albert Martin at the wheel. He moved to the door and opened it. Albert was apparently unconscious. The air bag from the steering wheel was shrinking.

Albert was a big man, fat around the midsection. A heavy red beard covered his fat face and a thick batch of red hair covered his fat head.

Shane turned slightly to press the fingers of his left hand against Albert's neck. The pulse throbbed under Shane's finger.

Albert's eyes popped open, and he turned toward Shane. The detective jumped back and the ground gave out beneath him. Shane fired his gun into the air as he fell backward, down the berm. His shoulders hit the ground before he rolled head over heels and landed on his hands and knees.

Shane shook his head and realized he had dropped his gun. Albert was out of the van and moving toward him with a knife in his hand. The detective pushed himself up and leapt to the side as Albert swung the knife wildly.

Then Albert turned and lowered his head like a bull preparing to charge. Shane saw his gun a few feet away and dove for it. He scooped it up as Albert ran at him. Shane fired once, the bullet hitting Albert in the throat. The big man stopped and clutched his neck. Blood flowed through his fingers.

Albert's eyes were empty when he looked at Shane. He took a step toward the detective, and Shane pulled the trigger on his gun, not realizing the slide had locked back and the gun was empty.

He prepared for an attack that never came. Albert took another step and fell to his knees. He stared at Shane for a moment before pitching, face first, into the ground.

Thirty minutes later, Shane was seated on the picnic bench in the grassy area.

David Palmer was seated across from him, his hands cuffed behind his back. He cried as Shane confronted him.

"Albert's dead."

Palmer nodded.

"Why did you kill Travis?"

Palmer shook his head. "Albert did."

Shane sipped some water. "Why did Albert kill Travis?"

"He found out what was going on. Albert was afraid he would tell the cops."

"What did Travis discover?"

Palmer laid it out for Shane, breaking into tears and sobs as he went along. Finally, when he was done he rested his head on the table.

"Final question. Why didn't you type Travis' suicide note in your office?"

"I didn't know Albert had killed Travis. I found out about it when Mark reported it to me."

Shane waved over Deputy Wolfe. "Take him and book him for murder," he said.

Palmer objected, but Shane got up and walked over to the Lieutenant.

"Did he say why they killed the kid?"

Shane nodded. "Yeah. It seems the camp was a middle point for a smuggling ring running contraband in and out of Canada."

"You mean marijuana?"

"Mostly, but according to Palmer, they were also bringing people across the border."

"Terrorists or illegals or what?"

Shane shrugged. "I don't know. Point is, they were into illegal trafficking, and the kid stumbled onto it. Martin and Palmer couldn't let that info get out, so they took care of the kid."

"Were both of them in on the killing?"

"Palmer denies helping, but he helped cover it up, so he's just as guilty."

The Lieutenant rubbed his chin as he thought. "Why were they doing that crap here, at a summer camp?"

"For that reason exactly. The two of them lived here year round. They could move dope or people or whatever else they wanted in that white van. What cop is going to pay that much attention to a summer camp van?"

"I guess that makes sense."

Shane stood up and watched three news vans pull into the parking lot. The group of kids was huddled in the far corner of the parking lot, still waiting for the camp to be opened. The news crews hustled over to the children with their microphones extended.

"Good luck," Shane said and clapped his hand on the Lieutenant's shoulder.

Shane McAfee walked down the path towards the clearing where Travis Nash had been found. He stopped and stared up at the branch from which the kid had hung. His own recollections of camp were light and airy. He knew two hundred kids would now be cheated of those memories.

The detective turned and stared at the late afternoon sun shimmering off the water. Hunger ached in his belly, and he knew several more hours of paperwork and bureaucratic red tape stood between him and a young woman he loved.

Death by Radio
By Barbara Curtis

For years everyone in Morgan Acres had regarded Margaret Winslow as a pleasant, spry, older lady. The worst that might be said of Margaret was that she could be a hazard to drivers on the narrow local roads when she took her after-dinner walks. That all changed the night she murdered her youngest nephew, Donald. Even more shocking was her complete lack of remorse. Reportedly her only comment as she was led away by two somber deputies was, "I do hope I'll be allowed to listen to my radio while I am imprisoned."

Margaret's venture down the road to crime began innocently enough on one of her evening walks. She and Donald had finished their evening meal of Thai noodles with tofu accompanied by two dried figs apiece. Margaret had taken care to explain the benefits of such healthy fare to Donald.

"There are twenty grams of protein in each serving and very low cholesterol!" she exclaimed. "As you approach thirty, you need to start thinking about these things."

Donald pushed the topping of bean sprouts to the side of his plate and cautiously put a forkful of noodles into his mouth.

"Whatever happened to meat loaf?" he mumbled.

"What, dear?"

"Nothing, Auntie," he said.

He continued pushing the noodles around, making little patterns on the white plate until Margaret excused herself and walked into the kitchen. Fearing what his aunt might consider a healthy dessert, Donald dumped the food from his plate into the garbage and headed upstairs.

"Thanks for dinner. I have to work on my reports," he called over his shoulder.

"Oh dear, I was just going to dish up the lemon and white bean puree. Well, I guess we can eat it later."

Margaret set the bowl back in the refrigerator and located her sturdy walking shoes. She checked the pocket of her nylon jacket for her radio and clipped her sunglasses to her regular eyeglasses. When not in use, the dark lenses stuck straight up, giving her the appearance of a large insect. She strode out the back door and walked along Smith Street at a steady pace.

Donald waited until she turned the corner before calling Domino's Pizza.

As was her custom, Margaret first concentrated on establishing a steady stride and even breathing. When she was walking comfortably, she inserted the earpiece and turned on her radio. She had walked nearly fifty feet before the music penetrated her consciousness. She recognized the bouncy opening notes of "The Teddy Bears' Picnic." Her face crinkled into a smile, and she was enveloped in a memory of lying on a braided rug in front of the cabinet radio listening to "Big Jon and Sparkie" while she played with her paper dolls.

Then, incredibly, she heard the voices of Jon Arthur and his puppet friend. Margaret pulled the small radio out of her pocket and checked the dial. It was tuned to the easy-listening station she always chose for walking. To Margaret's delight, the program continued with Ukie, the Cincinnati cab driver, joining in the action. So absorbed was she in following the adventures of the beloved radio characters that she walked a little farther than usual. The closing advertisement for "Pepsi Cola—more bounce to the ounce" was followed by silence.

Margaret stepped up her pace in her eagerness to return home and tell Donald what she had heard. She hurried up the back steps and into the kitchen.

"Donald! Donald, come downstairs!"

Donald quickly checked his waste basket to make sure he had left no traces of the pizza.

"Coming, Auntie," he called.

He found his aunt seated at the table cradling her little radio like it was a holy relic.

"You will never believe what I heard tonight!" Margaret said, eyes twinkling. "An entire episode of my favorite childhood radio show, 'Big Jon and Sparkie.' "

"Oh," Donald said.

"Of course you wouldn't know about radio shows, but it was such a pleasure to hear those marvelous voices."

"It was probably a special broadcast," Donald ventured.

"They even included the old advertisements without one interruption by the station," Margaret marveled.

"Umm." Donald turned away. "I really do need to complete the assignment for my statistics class."

Living here for free allowed Donald to afford tuition, but he had to put up with the mental meanderings and dreadful cooking of his aunt.

"Certainly, you get your work done. Maybe I'll just run next door to see if Vera Jean heard the show."

Margaret walked across the lawn and rapped sharply on her neighbor's front door.

"Hello, Margaret. Come on in."

Margaret stepped into the cluttered living room. She frowned briefly at the lingering odor of roast beef.

"Vera Jean, you'll never guess what I heard this evening! While I was walking I listened to an entire episode of 'Big Jon and Sparkie.' "

Vera Jean's eyes widened.

"Oh, my gosh! Wherever did you hear it? I'd nearly forgotten about that show."

"I just turned on my radio and there it was. It must have been a special broadcast."

"Do you think they will run it again? I'd like to hear it, too."

"I don't know. My radio was set to the easy listening station and it just came on."

Vera Jean turned her head to one side like a little bird.

"That's odd. I had my radio on the easy listening station while I washed up the dishes, but all I heard was regular music—Barry Manilow and Donny Osmond."

Margaret drew her brows together.

"Perhaps the dial got bumped when I put on my jacket. The channels must be close."

Vera Jean nodded. "That must be it. I'll listen for it tomorrow night. It surely would be a treat to hear that old show."

Margaret smiled. "You'd love it."

"Would you join Herb and me for dessert? I made peach pie and we've got ice cream to top it with."

Margaret shook her head. "No, thank you. I have dessert at home. I must be going."

She walked back to her own kitchen, reflecting on the poor eating habits of Herb and Vera Jean.

The next evening Margaret eagerly anticipated her walk. After a nice supper of roast squash and turnips, she hurried down the street. To her delight, "Big Jon and Sparkie" once again came through the earpiece. She was charmed by the gentle humor and small-town atmosphere of the episode. She quickened her pace to return home and recount the story to Donald.

"Donald?" she called upstairs. Perhaps he was too engrossed in his studies to hear her. Margaret returned to the kitchen and spotted Vera Jean backing her Buick down the adjoining driveway. Margaret hurried across the lawn.

"Did you hear it?" she asked eagerly.

Vera Jean frowned in puzzlement and shook her head.

"Both Herb and I tried all the channels and we couldn't find any trace of old radio shows. Are you sure it was a local station?"

"Well, I don't know," Margaret replied. "It came in just fine on my little radio."

The two women stared at each other until Margaret shrugged and said, "I'll let you know if I get any information about the broadcasts."

When Donald came downstairs to sneak out for a candy bar, he overheard his aunt on the telephone.

"Do you know if any other station has this kind of programming? I see. Yes, I'm aware that I can purchase recordings of old radio shows. Thank you for your time."

Margaret hung up and sat silently at the table. She didn't even hear Donald stumble over her gardening clogs as he went down the back steps. Margaret had always considered herself to be a sensible person. She puzzled over this quirk of nature that was bringing old broadcasts to her little radio. Finally, she threw up her hands, concluding that it was one of life's mysteries. The programs were a gift to her alone. It would never do to look a gift horse in the mouth, so she would accept these nightly treats and enjoy them to the fullest.

But Donald grew concerned enough to call his sister Carol in Sacramento.

"I think the old girl's cracking up," he said. "She thinks she's hearing radio broadcasts from 1953."

The ever-practical Carol replied, "If she's loony, you could get power-of-attorney over her affairs. She's got the house and there's undoubtedly a tidy sum in savings."

Donald shifted from one foot to the other. "It's not that. I'm just worried that she'll get hit by a truck because she's listening to imaginary radio shows instead of watching the traffic."

"In that case, you would wind up with her life insurance," Carol replied cheerfully.

Realizing that Carol wasn't sharing his level of concern, Donald promised to keep in touch, and said good-bye.

The following week he took his aunt grocery shopping at the local Safeway, hoping to sneak some cookies or chips into the cart.

"Do you suppose they carry White King soap?" Margaret asked.

"I don't know," Donald said.

"They advertised it on the radio last night. I'd forgotten how nicely it cleans clothes; much more gentle than harsh detergents." She hummed a little tune as she scanned the shelves in vain.

In the next aisle Donald managed to pick up a bag of barbecue potato chips while his aunt was looking for Ipana toothpaste.

"That Bucky Beaver and his Ipana was always so cute," she said.

Donald agreed whole-heartedly while he arranged some bags of vegetables over the top of the chips.

Margaret was so busy asking the bewildered clerk about long-extinct brands of syrup and cake mixes that she didn't even notice Donald's spurious food choices at the checkout.

That night Margaret was thrilled to hear the adventures of Gene Autry and his faithful companions at the Melody Ranch as she walked her usual route. She was so caught up that she returned to the house singing cowboy songs. She set her radio on the table, and went out the front door to set the sprinkler on the flower beds. That task completed, she stepped inside and stopped in the doorway. Donald had her radio in his hands, moving the frequency dial and listening through the earpiece.

"Donald James Winslow!" She lifted her chin and drew herself up to her full height of five feet, one-and-one-half inches. "You are not to handle my private possessions without permission."

Donald turned, stricken, and stammered, "I was just checking to see if...to see if you needed batteries."

"I am perfectly capable of changing batteries without your assistance."

She snatched back the radio and stalked into her bedroom.

For the next two nights, Margaret's evening walks were completed in silence. Not even static came through her radio. Donald was treated to glaring looks and an extremely sour rhubarb sauce at supper.

"Sugar just spoils the good rhubarb taste," Margaret declared, spooning an extra serving onto his plate.

On the third night, the broadcasts resumed with the Texaco Star Theater presenting Jack Benny and Dennis Day.

An uneasy truce settled between Donald and Margaret over the next several months. Twice she suspected he might have touched her radio, but there was no concrete proof. Donald observed Margaret spending more and more time in her easy chair muttering about Big Jon or Cinnamon Bear. She quit attending her garden club meetings and missed her appointment at the Cut N Curl for her twice yearly permanent wave. The day he spotted her laughing and talking to her radio characters while hanging out the laundry, he decided to act. Unfortunately, Donald was not an accomplished conspirator and made his phone call where Margaret could overhear.

"It has reached the point where she can't distinguish between fantasy and reality. I'm sure she can remain in her home if we just get rid of that radio."

Margaret clutched at the front of her shirt. Get rid of her radio! That was the moment she made her terrible decision.

Margaret made a quick visit to her gardening shed, and then cooked a batch of rhubarb sauce. She served Donald first. He grimaced at the taste, but quickly shoveled down his meal. She smiled at him and set out on her evening walk.

Following a delightful program wherein Hopalong Cassidy and his sidekicks, Lucky and California, tricked the bank robbers, she returned home, felt Donald's wrist for a pulse, and called the authorities to report a death.

It was quickly determined that the old lady was not fit to stand trial, and she was remanded to a mental facility. When six weeks had passed, Vera Jean could no longer bear the thought of Margaret languishing in that awful place with no visitors. Although she had never had occasion to set foot in a mental hospital, she knew her Christian duty.

The day she chose to visit Margaret, the dance class at the lodge auxiliary ran late, so she had to push the Buick above the speed limit to make it to Medical Lake on time. She blamed Elvira Palmer. That woman just could not understand three-quarter time.

Margaret was seated on a bench when Vera Jean arrived. She waved to her neighbor and motioned for her to sit down. Vera Jean took Margaret's hands in her own and said, "How are you doing?"

"I take regular walks around the grounds and I am taking the opportunity to educate the staff about the importance of a healthy diet," Margaret said. "The meals here need a great deal of improvement."

Vera Jean dropped Margaret's hands and nodded uncertainly. After a time she asked, "How long do you think you'll have to stay here?"

Margaret turned to face her in surprise. "Why, I reside here. I listen to my radio every evening. Just last night I heard the important message at the start of the Signal Oil program: 'I am the Whistler, and I know many things, for I walk by night. I know many strange tales, many secrets hidden in the hearts of men and women who have stepped into the shadows.' "

Firebug
By Dale Alling

What a sucktastic day. One of the most miserable feelings in the whole entire world is waking up from a nap in the middle of summer when it's hot and dry, and you're all sticky and your clothes are all twisted, and you have a headache from being dehydrated. You know that feeling? It's even worse when your leg is in a cast and you can't scratch that itch behind your knee. Ugh, I hated this weather. I had broken my leg, so I couldn't do drywall, that's my profession, drywaller for a general contractor, and so I was staying at my parent's place with my sister and my cousin. My parent's were gone on a cruise, some sort of second honeymoon. My sister Lucy was fifteen and my cousin Simon was seventeen, so it wasn't like they needed a babysitter. I think Mom and Dad just wanted me around to make sure they didn't burn the place down. Their house is on the north side of Spokane and the sky was hazy from forest fires to the north.

"Lucy! bring me a pop!" I yelled in the general direction of downstairs.

"Go get it yourself, Jerry!" she answered back.

"I'm a disabled cripple!"

"I don't see no handicap sticker hanging from your rear view, so get it yourself."

"If I fall down the stairs and break my other leg, I'm gonna sue."

"My attorney will be in touch. By the way, Evan is here."

Evan is my favorite hermit. We've known each other since high school, and even though he is a strange little weirdo, he's my best friend. I descended the stairs with the help of crutches and managed not to break my neck.

"Evan! what brings you out of your cave?" I flopped down on the couch next to him.

"Well, my internet and cable TV are down, so I had little choice."

"Hate to tell you, but it's down here, too. Called and they said they're working on it."

"Want to go mess around in the woods? Find some more paint balls?"

"It's too hot to go hiking. Not to mention my leg, Genius."

"Well, do you want to go rent a game or something?"

"I suppose. It's better than sitting here and staring at the static on the TV."

Lucy stuck her head around the door leading into the kitchen. "You need to feed the dog first."

"I fed the dog yesterday, you go do it."

"Noooo, I'm doing the dishes today."

"Well, get Simon to do it."

"Yeah right. He's still at work."

I hopped to my feet. "Fantastic. If I break my other leg feeding Rufus, I'm gonna sue." I hobbled out by the back door and scooped a cupful of dog food. Then I looked down at his dish. "Hey, his dish is still full."

Lucy walked over, her hands still soapy. "That's weird, the little fatty always cleans his bowl."

"Maybe Simon fed him before he left this morning."

"Maybe. Hey, have you even seen Rufus today?"

"I don't think so. You know how he crawls out under the fence. Ask Simon when he gets home. We're gonna run over to Hastings, get a game."

The video game failed to live up to the hype and made for a dull evening. Lucy was at a friend's house, and Evan went home. Unfortunately, it was after dark and Rufus was still nowhere to be found. I hopped up the stairs and knocked on the door to the spare bedroom. Simon answered the door.

"Hey, man, you seen the dog today?"

"Naw." Simon doesn't talk much.

"Did you see him yesterday?"

"Beats me. I've been at work."

Simon has been staying here at my parent's house this summer. His mom, my aunt, sent him over from the coast because of some sort of trouble at home, or some such thing. My parents mentioned it in passing, but I didn't catch the details. I don't know, he seems polite, and he's been getting up early for some job all summer, so he doesn't seem like a juvenile delinquent to me.

"All right, well, if he doesn't show tomorrow, can we drive over to the animal shelter, see if they picked him up?" My bum right leg has made it nearly impossible for me to drive.

"Yeah, I get off earlier tomorrow."

The next morning came and Rufus was still gone. Lucy was beginning to get agitated—even though she always claimed to hate "fat old Rufus," I suspect she has a soft spot for the mutt. Unfortunately, the pound had no half-dachshund, half-poodle, half-sewer-rat in holding, so we switched to plan B: fliers and interrogating the neighbors.

I don't know why I got stuck with flier duty, being the one with the broken leg and all. No way was I going to be able to cover the entire area, so I enlisted Evan to do half my work for me. It's not like he had anything better to do on his day off. Armed with a stapler and printouts featuring a picture of Rufus from last Christmas, I started papering telephone poles.

"Hi-De-Ho, neighbor," a voice behind me said. I turned around, and Terry Paulson was leaning over the wooden fence. Terry is our next-door neighbor. Well, he's the substitute neighbor. The house next door actually belongs to Reed Paulson. Terry has been house sitting for his uncle Reed this summer. Mr. Paulson has been over on the coast. Some sort of medical clinic, I don't know the details. Terry seems nice enough. He's usually in the driveway tinkering under the hood of his old Charger.

I walked over to the fence and flipped a flier in Terry's face. "Hey 'Wilson,' you seen our dog?" I asked. Terry held up the flier and made a show of squinting at the picture.

"Golly, I don't think so. Was he wearing the Santa hat at the time he disappeared?"

"Har har. Just let us know if you see him, okay? Hey, how's the car coming?" I knew better than to ask Terry about his car, but it slipped out. I spent the next twenty minutes listening to him talk about cam shafts and differentials. Never been much of a gear head myself.

Evan had no leads either, but being Evan, he had already started working the problem. See, sometimes he thinks he is a detective, but I think it depends on what book he is reading at the time.

"At this point, we have to consider kidnapping as a possibility," Evan said.

"Dognapping."

"What?"

"Dognapping. That's what they call it when it's a dog."

"Nevertheless, from what I understand, even though Rufus liked to escape, he was never one to wander, so a person could conclude that he was taken."

"That's just stupid. Who would want an old, ugly, fat little dog?"

"I'm not establishing motive here. I'm just laying out scenarios."

"Well, maybe it was you."

"Possibly; I did have opportunity."

"Plus, you give off a strange little weirdo vibe."

"Also would have been easy for me to muzzle Rufus, and sneak him out of your yard."

"Well, I don't really care, but my mom is gonna pitch a fit when she gets back."

"Have your parents called?"

"No, I don't know if they even can, since they're on a cruise. Anyway, I'll leave it up to my sister to tell them. She's the one who still lives here. I'm just visiting."

Lucy somehow managed to hear this from the living room and yelled back her two cents.

"Ha! I'm not telling Mom, you're the one in charge, remember?"

"I'll make sure you get the blame, Lucy. Hey! Evan wants to know who has a motive to kidnap and/or kill Rufus. Whatcha think?"

"It was probably you so you wouldn't have to feed him."

"Seriously."

Lucy thought for a moment. "Maybe it was the Bruno brothers."

The Bruno brothers. Of course, I should have suspected them right away. Hank and Frank Bruno live a couple blocks away, and they are the most evil, destructive sociopaths I've ever met. The scumbags have had it in for our family since I first met them. Dad called the cops on them a couple months ago when he caught them smoking pot in the vacant lot next door. I remember when I was in junior high, they slashed the tires on my mountain bike. They were three and five years old at the time.

I needed backup to confront the Brunos, so I yelled upstairs for Simon. Evan, Simon and I headed down the street as the sun was going down. Terry yelled down the street after us, "Hey, everything all right? Where you guys going?"

"We're going to go find some trouble!" I yelled over my shoulder. Actually, I hoped the kids weren't home.

Terry laughed and yelled back, "I used to look for trouble, too. I know better now. Keep my troubles on the down low."

The Brunos had the ugliest house on their block and their yard consisted of dry weeds sticking out from between several rusting cars. I crutch-hopped up to the door and banged on the screen. Evan and Simon looked nervous behind me. Evan is pretty non-confrontational, and Simon seems too well mannered to go around starting fights.

We waited on the porch for a couple minutes and knocked again. No answer, so I turned around. "Looks like they got lucky—"

"Hey!" I heard a voice yell. A teenager poked his head around the corner of the house. It was Frank. "Why don't you maggots get out of here?" Frank said, polishing a chrome rear-view mirror with a dirty rag. Except he didn't use that word. It rhymed with maggots though.

"Not so fast. I need you to tell me if you've seen our dog." I pulled a flier from my back pocket.

"If I saw something like that on our property, I'd shoot it," Hank Bruno said, walking up behind his younger brother.

"Why, hello, Hank, nice to see you all polite and rehabilitated since your last stint in juvie."

"Look, we ain't part of your neighborhood watch party, so why don't you and your boyfriends beat it?"

"I bet you know all about playing boyfriend at the juvenile correction center."

Hank stepped forward and spit on my leg cast. It didn't bother me much, all part of the tough guy dance, but I heard a yell behind me and turned to see Evan holding Simon back from leaping at Hank's throat.

"White trash has no right to live! I will make you pay! The right is gone! GONE!"

Simon was screaming gibberish, and his face was red as a beet. I don't think I had ever heard him raise his voice before. Hank stepped back with his hands held up.

"Whoa! We ain't seen your dog, Gimp. Now get out of here before we make you leave!" His brother Frank was now brandishing the rear-view mirror like a club.

"Easy now, easy. We're leaving." I spun around and high-tailed it down the street as fast as my crutches could carry me. Once we were back on our block, Evan spoke up.

"Well, that went fantastic, Jerry. Think we can get ourselves shot next time?"

"Eh, the Brunos are all talk," I lied. Actually, they seemed perfectly capable of shooting all three of us in cold blood.

"What I want to know is, what got into you, Simon?" I stared at my cousin, who was now breathing easier. He kept his eyes on the ground.

"Sorry, they got under my skin," he said, not looking up.

"Naw, it's cool. I've just never seen you freak out like that."

"I'm just tired. I gotta get up at like three for work tomorrow, so I'm gonna go to bed." Simon headed for the front door.

I turned to Evan. "Seriously, what do you think?"

"Besides nearly getting killed? I don't think they know anything. I don't think they would threaten to shoot the dog if they had already shot the dog."

"You got a point. Poor old Rufus probably just ran off and got hit by a car," I said.

Bright and early Wednesday morning, I heard screaming. I rolled off the bed and hit the floor. Hopping up, I started yelling down the stairs.

"What's going on? Lucy?"

"Rufus! Rufus is dead!"

It was just as I had feared. Somebody must have found him in a ditch by the road.

"Look, Luce, he just kept digging his way out of the backyard, it was only a matter of time."

As I came down the stairs, Lucy was pacing back and forth with her arms crossed. Her eyes said she had been crying. She looked at me.

"Rufus isn't just dead. He was burned up!"

"Wait, what? Burned?"

"I was looking in the woods, and I'm pretty sure it's him. You need to see this. Simon already left for work, didn't he? We should drive up the back road so you can see."

"I'm not driving my truck in this condition, and you can't drive stick. Let me call Evan."

It was a nasty sight when the three of us arrived at the clearing that was the location of Rufus' body. We could smell the burnt hair well before we saw his body.

"How do we know for sure it's Rufus?" Evan asked.

"Well, that looks like his collar. Pretty sure he didn't just run off."

"This is making me sick. I'm going to wait in the truck," Lucy said.

"Okay, Lucy. We'll put him in the garbage bag, bring him back to bury."

"All right Evan," I said after Lucy left. "Who would burn the dog alive?"

"Actually, we don't know if Rufus was alive when he was torched."

"How do we find out—perform a dogtopsy?"

"You can if you want, but I'm not going to. Look, let me do some research on this. It's pretty sick stuff."

"Looks like this isn't the first fire up here. I see a couple other places there are fire pits."

"Fairly recent, too. I'm guessing the dog wasn't the first victim, either. That looks like a rat or a squirrel skeleton in the ashes over there."

"Sick dog burning aside, it's too hot and dry to be starting fires up here this time of year."

"Yeah. They have several fires going up on the reservation."

"All right, help me scoop up the remains."

We had a small ceremony in the back yard and Rufus was buried under his favorite tree. I made Simon dig the grave because I didn't want dirt to slip inside my cast.

Evan came back later, while I was eating lunch. He was carrying several pages he had printed out off of web sites.

"Did your internet start working again?"

"No, I hacked into my neighbor's wifi so I could get online."

"How virtuous. So what's the deal?"

"I think what we are dealing with here is a classic pyromaniac."

"As opposed to new school pyromaniac?"

"As opposed to an arsonist. Arsonists burn for for criminal reasons: sabotage, vandalism, insurance scam, etcetera."

"Okay, right. Spokane's had some warehouses torched."

"This, on the other hand, seems more personal. The perpetrator burned the subjects for no apparent gain."

"They could have killed Rufus out of spite or revenge."

"But not the burned up squirrels. They were burned before Rufus."

"So he was working his way up to bigger and better things? Well, that's just plain creepy. Psychotic criminal behavior makes me think Bruno brothers again."

"I don't know. If that was the case, both of them were hiding it really well. I'm going home to do more research. Make sure your smoke alarms are working."

So there I was. It was still hot, my leg hurt and now I ran the risk of being burned alive by some firebug. I really didn't want to tell Mom that her dog was dead, and the parents were going to be home in a few days. Plus, I just wasted an hour jumping through hoops on the phone.

Lucy walked in the front door and stood in front of the air conditioner.

"So I called the police," I said.

"What'd the police say?" Lucy asked, angling her sweaty head in front of the cold air.

"They told me to call the Department of Fish and Wildlife, who had me call the fire district."

"Well, it *is* fire season."

"And they put me in touch with Animal Protection Services, where I left a voice mail."

"I guess that's bureaucracy at work," Lucy said.

"Tell me about it. This whole pyromaniac on the loose thing is freaking me out."

"It reminds me of when we had the serial killer in town."

"Yeah, but he was targeting prostitutes only. A pyromaniac is just looking for something flammable."

"Great. Last time I checked, I'm flammable," said Lucy.

"Look, even though a dead dog is apparently not enough to get homicide investigators involved, me and Evan are working the case."

"I feel soooo much safer."

"Our next step is making a suspect list."

"People who came in contact with Rufus?"

"And who would choose to do their burning up on the hill, in the woods."

"Well, *you* always hated Rufus."

"I did not! Obviously the Bruno brothers are on the list."

"Wait, I just remembered something. You know Reed Paulson?"

"Yeah. Terry is house sitting for him, cause he's over on the coast in a hospital."

"Do you know why he's in the hospital? He's receiving treatment for extensive burns."

This was a twist. I didn't expect the *good* neighbors to be involved.

"So, what are you thinking, Terry set his uncle on fire?" I asked.

"What? No, no, obviously Mr. Paulson burned himself during one of his acts of arson!"

"So he snuck out of the hospital, came back to town and killed our dog?"

"To feed his sick and twisted fire needs!"

"This is blowing my mind. I need to text Evan."

Evan was busy playing World of Warcraft and couldn't be bothered until his raid was over. Being the man of action that I am, I decided to drag Simon along when I went next door to confront Terry. He took a little convincing, but we finally knocked on the Paulson's front door. I didn't really have a plan, but I wanted to read Terry's reaction when confronted with the evidence and hoped he wasn't packing a flame thrower.

"Hey there, Jerry, what's the haps?" Terry asked. "I saw you digging in your yard today.

Whatcha doing?"

"Our dog is dead. We buried him."

"Geez, that's terrible. I'm sorry."

"We found his carcass up in the woods. He was burned."

"Oh, no! That's awful! What happened?" No odd reaction from Terry so far.

"Don't know, but I'm going to find out. I wanted to ask you about your uncle."

"Uncle Reed? He's over on the coast for rehabilitation—skin grafts."

"So he was burned? Like Rufus?"

"Well, kinda...but it was a chemical burn at his job."

"Wait, chemicals? Not flames?" I felt stupid.

"Look, Jerry, sorry that your dog died. I need to go check on dinner before it sets off the smoke alarm."

"Uh, have a good night, Terry." I said. He closed the door.

I turned to Simon. "Well, that was extremely awkward. Did you know it was a chemical burn? I didn't know it was a chemical burn."

Simon shrugged his shoulders. I got the impression he was tired of me dragging him around the neighborhood to accuse people. "I'm going to bed, I got to get up at three thirty for work," he said.

Since I struck out again, I called Evan.

"Not now, I'm tanking Kel Thuzad," he said, still playing the game.

"Who? Look, strike two in our suspect list. What else have we got?"

"I don't think we have an official suspect list. Buff Threevan."

"I don't even know what you're saying. You were going to do some more research. What did you find out?"

"You're going to make us wipe!" Games were always more important to Evan than reality. "Look, two things. Do you know what zoosadism is?"

"I could probably make a guess."

"Zoosadism is pleasure from cruelty to animals. Research shows serial killers often start by torturing and killing small things like bugs, then small animals, and eventually, people. Our suspect was burning rodents and is now burning dogs. That shows a pattern of escalation." Over the phone I could heard the sounds of gaming disaster coming from his speakers. "Great! We are all dead!" he said, confirming my suspicions.

"Yeah," I told him, "and if this guy escalates to people, we could be dead, too."

"Well, right now our guild just died fighting the boss. Thanks for the distraction."

"Never mind the game, what's the second thing?"

"I went back up to the crime scene to poke around. There were about a dozen different fire pits in the general vicinity of where we found Rufus. I'm no expert, but they all looked fairly recent, within the last month or so."

"So if there has been a dozen fires up there this summer, why haven't we seen any smoke?"

"Exactly what I thought. Whoever is doing this must do it while it's still dark. You can't see the clearing from the houses, so the light of the fire wouldn't be given away."

"Maybe we should stake out the clearing."

"Not tonight, I'm tired from playing WoW. Hey, did you know pyromania is pretty rare? It usually exhibits itself in young males, and they sometimes derive sexual satisfaction from watching their target burn. It's called pyrophillia. They also don't set something on fire and leave, they get the enjoyment from watching the burning."

"Fantastic. Look, I'm going to load one of my dad's shotguns and set it next to my bed tonight. Home invasion laws mean I can shoot anyone who comes inside the house, right?"

"I don't think it's supposed to work quite like that. Besides, couldn't they just set your house on fire from the outside?"

I hung up on Evan at that point. What if they got rid of Rufus so he wouldn't bark while they were spraying gasoline on the side of our house tonight? I knew I wasn't going to sleep well.

One of the most miserable feelings in the whole entire world is waking up in the middle of the night and it's still hot and dry even though the sun has gone down, but you still have goosebumps because you're creeped out that you are next on a pyro's hit list. I dragged myself to the bathroom for a drink of water. Things looked normal. I decided to peek into Lucy's room. Lucy wasn't there.

I looked at the clock. It was three-fifteen in the morning. I checked downstairs and looked outside, still no Lucy. I was getting nervous now. I yelled, but no answer. I went back upstairs and banged on Simon's door. It was about time for him to get up, anyhow. No answer. I opened the door and looked inside. His bed was empty as well. I didn't think he left for work until four, so why was he already gone? I had a sick feeling in my stomach. Grabbing the shotgun from my room, I headed for the woods.

I saw the light of a fire as I struggled up the hill with my crutch. I dropped to my belly and began crawling. The clearing came into view and I saw two figures next to a fire. Lucy was lying on the ground in her pajamas with her hands behind her back. She was bound and gagged.

The person standing beside her turned around. It was Simon. He was holding a can of gasoline which I recognized from my dad's garage. In the fire, I could see a pair of shoes. Simon stared at the fire. He had a look in his eyes that I had never seen before. It was earnest, like he wanted something from what he was looking at, but it was far away at the same time. Stupidly, I had forgotten my phone. It was up to me.

As I crept closer, Simon shoved Lucy further away from the fire with his foot. She didn't squirm. She must have been unconscious. He carefully began to pour gas around the edge of her body. He was making a spiral pattern inward, and gasoline began to soak her clothes. He finished and set the gasoline can behind him. Reaching into his pocket, he pulled out a barbecue lighter.

It was now or never. I hopped up with my crutches and pumped a shell into the chamber. It was loud enough that Simon heard it. I decided to play it calm.

"Simon, what are you doing?" I asked, holding the shotgun at my shoulder but pointed towards the ground.

He looked up at me and squinted into the darkness. "I—I have to do it Jerry, I have to. I have to. Have to."

"You don't have to do anything, Simon. You didn't have to burn the dog, and you don't have to burn my sister."

"I need it. I need to see it. I have to set the fire!"

"If you set her on fire, I'm going to kill you. You know that, don't you, Simon?"

"Do you think I would do it if I didn't have to? The pressure! You do not know what this pressure is!"

"Stop it right—"

"Pressure is screaming behind my eyeballs! Eyeballs full of blood! Brain is going to explode! I have to! *HAVE TO!*"

Simon started turning in a circle, clutching the sides of his head and staring at something a million miles away. He still had the lighter in his hand and was flicking it off and on. One false move would set the gasoline ablaze.

I really didn't want to shoot my cousin, but he wasn't exactly listening to reason. I pointed the barrel at his legs and prepared to fire.

In one swift motion, the gasoline can came out of the darkness, swung and hit him in the back of the head. He pitched forward and fell chest first into the fire. He screamed in pain and rolled away, beating at his burning shirt. The gas can swung again down on the top of his head and he stopped moving. Lucy stood over him holding the now dented can.

"Lucy! get away from the fire!" I yelled. She was still soaked in gasoline.

"Is he dead?" she asked after she pulled the tape off her mouth.

I sat down on the ground and felt his pulse. "Still alive," I said. "Are you okay?" Lucy sat down next to me and stared at Simon. She didn't say anything for several minutes.

"He has a jug of water over there," she finally said. "We should put this fire out before the whole place goes up."

"I guess this explains why he was getting up so early," I said.

"Not to mention the trouble he was getting into that got him sent over here," she said.

The sun was coming up as we tied Simon's hands and feet. He wasn't very good at tying knots himself because Lucy had been able to slip out of the ropes while I had confronted him. For somebody who cried when Rufus died, I hadn't seen her crack one bit during this whole ordeal. She was a tough girl.

In my condition Simon was too heavy to carry, so we dragged him by his feet down the trail to the neighborhood. Halfway there Lucy stopped.

"Wait a second," she said and she pulled his shoes off his feet.

"Crazy idiot burned up my shoes." She slipped his sneakers on her feet, and we continued down the trail.

The Vacation
By Steve Oliver

Spokane, 1964

I had a great life from the time I got out of high school until I was in my early thirties. I had lots of money and broads and friends. Some of the friends were in the same business I was—holdup man. I hit liquor stores all over the San Fernando Valley for about two years without a single arrest.

Then I moved to San Diego for awhile and hit them there. I moved around to other cities, too, mostly in Southern California and Arizona—I liked the weather. I also made a little money as a salesman from time to time, just in case anyone had any questions about my means of support. I thought my life was charmed until I hit a little store in Beaumont, California, and in about five minutes I was surrounded by all three cars of their police force. For that little crime, I was duly sentenced and shipped off to the state facility at Vacaville, where I learned how to make license plates. When I got out, I was forced to make a plan that would get me out of the hair of the state of California, and the best thing I could figure was to allow my family to take pity on me and let me live with them. My brother Randall and his wife Glenda and my mother had moved to a place called Spokane, Washington, where my little brother had managed somehow to get his hands on a restaurant which made a lot of money. So I took my parole papers and one hundred dollars and two sets of clothes, and duly reported for work.

Now, my brother could have made me a manager or assistant manager or even given me a job as a waiter, but according to him, I didn't have the experience for any of those things. So what does he do—he makes me a dishwasher. And not even the top dishwasher, but an assistant to Sam the dishwasher, who is from Pakistan or some place.

Well, my mother had a heart condition, and everyone in the family said that if I did anything bad, it could kill her, and I did feel ashamed that I had embarrassed them, even though I knew I had a good reason for what I had done. Sam told me how to wash dishes, and when we had slack time I also bused the dishes, which I liked because now and then I could make eye contact with some nice-looking babe who was in the restaurant with her family. And once in awhile even caught the eye of some good looking dish who was with her date.

Still, I wasn't getting rich, and I wasn't getting any pussy. After all, who wants to go out with a guy who doesn't have any money and doesn't have a car? I asked my brother to loan me his precious car once or twice, but since it was a 1964 Impala with chrome wheels and a 409 engine, I guess I wasn't good enough to drive it.

He said that if I kept my nose clean, he would co-sign a loan for me if I bought something sensible like a Rambler or a bottom-of-the-line Plymouth—ten years old. I didn't say anything at the time, because there was usually no point in talking to him, but *that* pissed me off.

Here was my baby brother, a kid I had hardly paid attention to when we were growing up, telling me that if I stayed clean he would help me get a crummy old car that I didn't even want. When the money was rolling in when I was in California I'd had several sports cars, the kind of car you didn't even see around Spokane.

But like I said, I didn't say anything. There was no use arguing. He knew he was in charge, and he acted like I was the little brother, and he was giving me a little payback for how I had treated him and how he thought I was treating mom. I knew he was wrong about that, about mom. I was still her favorite. I always had been. Whenever I gave her a hug she always whispered, "You're my favorite, Ronnie. You'll always be my favorite. You were my first born." That was something I didn't tell Randall, either. No point in that.

So I bided my time. I didn't know what I was waiting for. I didn't know what would happen. I just knew something had to happen, because I couldn't stand this forever. I couldn't be a dishwasher forever. And I couldn't see where I would go from here. What was I going to become— a waiter? Was I going to manage my brother's restaurant? I couldn't see a guy like me, a guy who'd had money and broads and big scores, ending up like that. It was a death sentence. Right here in Spokane.

What set me off was when Sammie told me that my brother was leaving for a week in Hawaii. I didn't even learn it from my brother. I got the information from the head dishwasher, who was my boss. Randall and Glenda had been planning it for awhile without letting anyone know but the manager and mom. So now in the middle of winter while I'm washing dishes in Spokane with no money and no car, my brother and his wife are getting on a jet, and flying to Hawaii to sit on the beach in Honolulu for a week.

The only thing he said to me before he left was, "You take care of the house while we're gone and stay out of trouble."

"Yeah sure," I said, making sure by the way I said it that he knew how I felt about it without actually saying anything.

The next morning, a cab came for them early and Randall was in such a good mood, he said, "Have a good time," as they walked out the door while I sat at the kitchen table drinking coffee and smoking a cigarette. "Have a good time," he said, like I was the one going on a trip.

I sat there awhile before I went to the cupboard and took out the bottle of Seagrams. I poured half a glass and drank it with my coffee. Then I tossed the coffee and just drank the whisky.

I started to feel like my old self. For the first time in a long time, I felt good. I continued to drink as I showered and dressed. I put on nicer clothes than I usually wore to work, a nice pair of slacks and a white shirt. Then I decided not to go to work. I found one of my brother's ties and a sports jacket. I got my best overcoat.

I hadn't decided on what I was going to do until I saw the box on the shelf of the closet. I knew about it, of course, but I hadn't thought of it for a while. It was a gun, a .38. My brother had bought it for protection. I took the box down and opened it. I handled the gun for awhile. Then I searched for shells and loaded it. It didn't have a holster and I didn't need one. I put it into my coat pocket where it felt good and right. I felt good. Better than I had in a long time.

I went to my brother's bedroom and looked at his car keys, but I didn't take them. I went to the kitchen and opened a cupboard door. He had a bunch of spare keys there on hooks. There were two extra car keys. I took one of them and closed the cupboard.

Now I felt even better.

I filled my flask with the Seagrams and put the bottle back in the cupboard. Then I went to the garage and started the car. I drove around for awhile, drinking from the flask and wondering what I would do.

It was afternoon in Spokane in January. I decided to have a few drinks, so I stopped at some bars on my way up Division Street, and I stopped at some more on my way down. I had a friendly chat with a few bartenders, but nothing more than that, and I was getting pretty drunk, so about five, I stopped and had a meal at the Pine Shed.

After that I went down the street to another bar. I had one drink and persuaded the bartender to sell me a pint to take with me—for a price.

I drank it as I cruised around some more, remembering the old days and what my life had been like when it was fun—before the state of California had interfered. If I'd been there I would have known what to do—hit a bunch of liquor stores.

But here they had state-owned stores, and I didn't like the idea of that. I didn't know how much money they had, or if they had guards, or what.

I drove around looking at the convenience stores that seemed to be on about every corner in the little neighborhoods.

I decided to try one that looked pretty prosperous, and it went better than I had expected. The store was empty, and the clerk was young and green and just said, "Yes, sir," when I told him to hand over the money. He emptied the cash register of a little over a hundred dollars, and I locked him in a little utility room with a padlock that was conveniently left hanging on the door jamb.

I drove across town, wanting to be as far away as possible when the police report came in. I tried to come up with a plan. What was I doing? Maybe if I went home, I could just forget about it, say I had an adventure and go back to work.

But I wasn't feeling like going back to work. I was like a kid on Halloween who's visited the first house. I wasn't ready to quit.

I stopped in at the Viking, and had a drink, and asked the bartender for a phone book. I called the train station and asked about train times out of town. There was a train to Chicago leaving in an hour.

Now I had a plan.

When the bartender came back to see if I wanted another drink, I handed him the phone book and pointed the pistol at him. The place was empty except for me and one other guy way down at the end of the bar.

"That's not very friendly," said the bartender.

"I'm sorry about this," I told him. "I like the bar, and you make a good drink, but I need the money."

He emptied the cash register, and I paid for my drink with a twenty from the bundle. That gave him an eighteen dollar tip.

"Thanks," I said, and left.

This time I didn't waste any time getting out of there. The bartender wasn't locked up, and he was probably phoning the police as I was leaving the parking lot.

I had been around town long enough and had noticed enough stores and bars that I had a pretty good idea where I would go. I hit four places by the time I got to the train station.

I almost hit a fifth place, but when I went in, there were too many people and I was getting pretty nervous—you only have so much luck.

I parked the car at a downtown parking lot, pulled the ignition wire out from under the dash and stripped the wires with my pocket knife so it would look like it had been hot-wired. I thought about the gun for a few minutes, wondering whether to take it with me, then finally decided to leave it. I stuffed it between the cushions of the back seat, figuring that I would retrieve it later and put it back in the closet.

When the train started moving, it was already midnight, but I couldn't sleep because I was feeling too alive, feeling like I did early on Friday night when the party was just starting. I went to the bar car and ordered a shot and a beer and lit a cigarette and talked to the colored bartender until this redhead came into the bar. She was already drunk from the way she walked unless she just wasn't used to the train movement. I sent a drink over to her, which the bartender delivered after giving me a wink.

Some girls don't like that sort of thing, but the moment she got the drink she smiled at me and raised her finger in a beckoning motion. I went to her table.

She was just my type. She wasn't afraid of living. She didn't want to know if I was safe or if I was going to call her in the morning, not like those broads in Spokane. She said she was from Chicago, had been visiting her sister and was on her way home. She said living in Spokane must be like being sent to hell and told me she hadn't had a dime's worth of fun in the two months she'd been stuck there.

We got down to some serious drinking then, both of us switching to straight whisky. What a great broad she was, that red hair, those green eyes, a great smile and a better laugh. And she was wearing a short skirt just past her knees and a white blouse and little diamond earrings. I was wondering what I would do with a great broad like this when all I had was a coach seat all the way to Chicago which I didn't even want to admit to her because it didn't make me sound like much, not the restaurant owner that I claimed to be.

She could have been reading my thoughts because about fifteen minutes before the bar closed she said, "I have a compartment."

I replied, "I'll see if I can get a bottle."

So I paid the bartender for two bottles of a medium grade whisky in a brown paper bag, and the party continued.

I think I was in love with that broad. I mean,

she was ready for anything. And funny. And what a great body. She smelled good, and she felt good, and the only bad thing about the whole experience was that those train beds weren't exactly made for what we were doing.

We got up about noon, and I sent for some food and bribed the porter to bring us another bottle. We kept on partying and talking and having sex. By the second day of the trip, I was beginning to worry about money, but I wouldn't be much of a guy to complain about this to a woman—it wouldn't take me where I wanted to go with her—so I didn't say anything and kept paying the bills. But I did wonder what I would do when we got to Chicago. If we were going to stay together I was going to have to get some money. I didn't have the gun anymore, and I didn't have enough money to buy another one. If I got a job as a dishwasher it was going to take me a long time to buy another gun.

We got into Chicago on the morning of the third day. I was still thinking about what I would do for money and a job as we were leaving the train. We were still a little tipsy after having been up almost all night drinking and screwing and making promises and talking about the future. I was carrying her bags, and she hadn't even asked me any questions about why I didn't have any luggage. I was wondering what would happen when we got to a cab stand. Would we get a cab together and go to her house or apartment? We had talked a lot about loving each other and having a good time in Chicago, but I didn't know much about her, where she worked and where she lived. I was still thinking about this when, as we walked down the aisle toward the entrance, she turned around and leaned up for me to kiss her. After I did, she said, "Honey. I have a husband."

"Oh, yeah?" I said.

"Yeah," she answered. "He's meeting the train."

"Oh."

"I can see him through the window."

"What do you want me to do?"

"Just don't be mad at me, baby."

"I ain't mad."

"I loved being with you, baby. Maybe we can do it again."

"Sure."

And that was that, except for me pretending I was just a guy on the train who had agreed to help her with her bags. Her husband was a nice-looking blond guy wearing a gold-colored camel-hair coat. He reminded me of my brother, prosperous, confident and sober.

But I wasn't sober and I wasn't prosperous. I was in Chicago in the middle of the winter, and I only had eight bucks on me. After losing my girl, I wanted to go get a drink but I didn't want to spend any more money until I had a plan. I was walking by a pipe shop when I got one.

I went into the shop and looked at a bunch of cheap pipes until I saw one that would do the trick. Then I went to a big drug store and bought some liquid shoe dye.

I found a place in the train station waiting area where I would be left alone and used the dye to blacken the pipe, then stood around smoking cigarettes until it dried enough so I could handle it. I put it in my pocket and checked the train schedule. There was a train leaving for Seattle late that evening.

I spent the rest of the day killing time and

casing stores around the station. Within a six-block area, I found about a dozen liquor stores, just the kind of places I needed, businesses with a large cash flow that were slow to deposit the money.

About an hour before train time, I started out on a route I had planned earlier, looking for a store that was empty except for the clerk. The very first one was being run by an old bald guy wearing a brown sweater and a big wart on the side of his nose. He looked up from the *National Enquirer* over his half-glasses and said, "Can I help you, sir?"

"Yeah. Stop calling me 'sir,' and give me the cash out of the drawer." I was pointing the "barrel" of the pipe at him, careful to keep most of it hidden inside the sleeve of my coat. I've robbed a lot of people, and I know that most of it is attitude. You sound like you mean it, you sound like you know what you're doing, and they do what you say. He barely glanced at the "gun," before punching the key on the cash register that opened it, pulling the cash out of the slots and handing it to me.

"What's under the cash tray?" I asked, and with a sigh he pulled the tray out and fished a couple of fifties and a hundred out and gave them to me.

I pointed behind him and said, "Give me two bottles of the McNaughton and a Seagrams."

He started to hand them over, and I said, "Put them in a bag." He did. I said, "Thanks," and left the store.

I had been so lucky that I decided not to do another store. I headed to the station.

The trip back was a little different from the trip out. I drank, but I didn't meet a broad. I had my memories: I thought about what a great dame she had been, how she had felt, what it felt like to feel like a big man, one who could have such a great broad. I went over the trip in my mind as I drank and watched the scenery go by.

The train, as it always seemed to, arrived in the middle of the night. I went to the Hotel Pedicord, got a room and slept in a bed for a change. In the morning, I reported to the restaurant.

"Where the hell have you been?" Bernie would have punched me, I think, if he thought he could have gotten away with it.

"I got sick."

"You couldn't call?"

"I was really sick."

"I ought to tell your brother."

"Is he back?"

"No. Tomorrow." He looked at me for a minute like he was deciding something. I knew what he was thinking. He wanted to fire me. He wanted to tell me to go to hell. He knew that my brother might not go for that.

"Get to work," he said finally.

"Sure, Bernie," I said, and took off my coat and headed for the kitchen.

My brother got back the next day.

I kept my nose to the grindstone and pretended that the boss wasn't my brother.

After Chicago and the broad, I guess I had it out of my system for a while. The dish water felt warm and good compared to the snow and cold outside, and listening to Sammie jabber didn't bother me at all. At night I went to my brother's house and stayed in my room and at dinner I said very little, which seemed to suit him fine. On the second night home he asked me about the car.

"Did you know my car was stolen?"

I looked surprised, like an actor looks surprised. "No. The Chevy?"

"Yeah, my Impala." He was really annoyed. That car was his baby.

"Jeez, Ron. I'm sorry to hear that. How'd it happen?"

"I was hoping you could tell me."

I shrugged. "How would I know? I didn't even know it was gone."

"It's kind of unusual for a car to be stolen out of a garage."

"I guess it is."

Glenda watched us from the counter where she was preparing dessert.

Ron studied me as he lit a cigarette. Then his eyes dropped, and Glenda told him to put out the cigarette until they finished the dessert.

Later, he said that the police had found the car and it had some damage. It was in the shop, and he was having to use Glenda's Falcon until it got fixed. He didn't seem to suspect me any more, and he could tell something about my attitude had changed. For now, I was grateful that he was my brother and that he was watching out for me and I had a place to stay. I'd had enough adventure for a while, and if I got restless again, I knew where the gun was.

An Act of Mercy
By Barbara Curtis

Susan considered her reflection in the glass of the lobby with satisfaction. She wore a red velvet dress with a rhinestone clasp, displaying strong shoulders and a generous swell of cleavage. She finished her drink, picked up her evening bag and made her way up the wide staircase. Her seat was in the front row of the balcony of the new Spokane Opera House. She settled into place and opened her program. This was where she'd met Paul, sitting in adjacent seats in the "golden circle."

She glanced at the empty seat next to her and then fixed her attention on the stage, where the orchestra had begun tuning. It felt nice to wear attractive clothing, though she really shouldn't have spent the money on the dress. She had cashed in everything to pay for David's rehab at St. Luke's. After four years, things were very tight.

Just as the lights dimmed, Paul slipped into his seat with an apologetic smile. He gave the red dress a quick, appreciative look and then concentrated on the opening notes of Verdi's

"Requiem." As he took off his coat their arms brushed, but Susan kept her eyes on the stage.

The full sound of orchestra and chorus enveloped her. The season ticket had been a gift from David's elderly parents in Phoenix. Susan had accepted it because she loved music, and because symphony concerts were something she and David had not attended together.

They lay together in Paul's bed. He turned and stroked her hair.

She sighed. "Don't you think it's strange that my marriage vows still mean something to me?"

"No, I think it's a measure of character."

"David suffers, you know. Sometimes I think it would be a blessing for him to go; to slip away in his sleep."

They lay together in the darkness. After a few minutes he spoke, "I could help with that."

He felt her body stiffen, and she turned to face him. He went on, "Only if you want help. I have access to the hospital pharmacy."

Susan sat up and put her head in her hands.

"I just don't know," she said softly.

Paul placed his hands on her shoulders. "You don't have to decide now."

He rubbed her neck and then wrapped his arms around her. When he felt her relax, he said, "The next concert isn't until December second. That's nearly three weeks away. Could we meet for dinner next week?"

"I'm just not ready to take that step."

"Would you meet me before the concert for dinner or drinks?"

"We could meet for drinks in the lobby," she conceded.

"All right. How about seven fifteen? That should give us time to be in our seats before the first piece."

She began to gather her clothing. "I really have to get home now."

Susan carefully fastened the rhinestone clasp at the front of her dress. She brushed her hair and applied lipstick. When she left Paul's townhouse, she looked as immaculate as she had entering the Opera House.

In the morning Susan woke at six. Unable to go back to sleep, she wrapped herself in an old flannel robe and made coffee. She sat down in the rocker and looked out at the trees. She had given up the house two years ago, but the apartment at least had a yard with evergreens. She drew the robe up to her face and inhaled. It had been David's, and even after numerous washings, she imagined it bore traces of his scent. Cradling a second cup of coffee Susan stared out the window and wondered if she had the courage to administer an overdose of medication.

At eight o'clock, she dressed and took her checkbook to the table. The portion of David's medical expenses not covered by insurance was taking every last penny. Ironically, they had purchased generous life insurance policies when they married, but hadn't planned for an accident that would leave one of them clinging to life. She calculated her bank balance and wrote out the rent check, then headed for the apartment office.

Two girls braked their bikes to a stop. "Hi, Mrs. Rowland. Like our new coats?"

"How pretty. Purple must be your favorite color."

They giggled.

"You have fun. Pretty soon we'll have snow and you'll have to put your bikes away."

"Yeah, I know," the older one said solemnly. "Bye."

Susan watched them gain speed, the younger one's front wheel wobbling. She missed being around kids. She could no longer put in the hours that teaching school required, so she'd accepted twenty hours a week at the library. Most of those hours she sat in a cubicle and rarely got to visit the children's section.

The bell on the door clanged as she stepped into the manager's office.

"Good morning, Mrs. Rowland."

It was Mrs. Stolberg. Susan had hoped to see Mr. Stolberg sitting behind the desk. She handed the woman her check and stood with her arms folded.

"How's your poor husband?" Mrs. Stolberg didn't wait for a reply. "So young for such a tragedy. Doctors these days are amazing. They can keep you alive forever. Of course they can't bring your poor husband back to normal."

"Hmm," Susan murmured and reached for the receipt.

"Well, you're young. You know, by the time I was your age, I had five children."

Susan pushed the door open without a word. She leaned against the building with her eyes closed. Maybe this would all be easier if she did have children, but she and David had decided to wait, and there was no changing that now.

Inside her apartment she sat down in front of the phone. She couldn't put off calling David's parents any longer. If she was going to go through with her plan, it was important that they would remember her phone call.

"Hello, it's Susan," she began.

"Oh, Susan, how's the weather in Spokane?" Mr. Rowland said in his booming voice. "Wonderful weather we're having. We don't regret moving south, I can tell you."

Susan sighed. It would be up to her to turn the conversation to David.

"I'm glad you're able to enjoy the weather," she said. "I have made some new care provisions for David. He'll be changing rooms next week."

"Oh?" David's father asked cautiously.

"I've made arrangements for him to be moved to the south wing where he can be monitored more closely."

When there was no answer, she went on.

"It's a bit more expensive, but Dr. Kernowsky believes that he should have that level of care."

She could almost see the older man's shoulders slump. He cleared his throat.

"Whatever you think is best. Mother and I appreciate how you look after our boy."

"I just wanted you to know right away. I'll mail you the specifics of the care plan."

"Yes, you do that."

After a silence they said goodbye.

Susan rummaged through her purse and stuffed some bills into her pocket. She spent the fifteen-minute walk to the Donut Parade lost in thought. She selected a fresh maple bar and a steaming coffee which she took to a window table. A tiny white-haired woman at the next table glanced her way. She smiled politely at Susan and then placed both papery hands around her coffee cup. When Susan had finished her maple bar the woman spoke. "You have a beautiful voice," she said.

Susan set down her coffee.

"You haven't sung on Sundays for quite awhile."

"No, I haven't."

The woman fastened her coat and walked to Susan's table.

"I will pray for you," she said.

Susan looked into her pale blue eyes. "Thank you," she said quietly.

It had been four years since she had sung at St. Aloysius Church. Four years ago, she couldn't have imagined drinking her Saturday coffee alone. Four years ago she couldn't have imagined that she'd consider taking a life, either. She finished her coffee and headed back to the apartment.

Two young women were working the YWCA front desk. Susan took out her membership card and placed it on the counter. The blonde with the ponytail hung up the phone and spoke to her partner.

"The van's pulling around now. They'll bring the wheelchair through to the men's locker room."

"Is it the guy who can't talk?"

"Yes, that's the one."

Susan gripped the pen tighter as she signed her name.

"I don't know if he gets anything out of this."

"It's good for his muscles, whether he's aware or not," the blonde stated.

Susan entered the locker room without a backwards glance. It was still difficult to hear David described as helpless and non-communicative. He had always been vibrant, the first one you noticed when you entered a room.

She pulled on her bathing cap, selected one of the roped-off lanes and entered the water. She swam steadily for several minutes. When she paused to adjust her cap, she saw David being lowered into the pool in a canvas harness. She smiled at him. It was just a reflex on her part, as she knew he wouldn't respond. Only once she thought she'd seen a flash of recognition in his eyes. Susan resumed swimming while the therapist moved David's legs through the prescribed motions. With each lap, her resolve strengthened.

After half an hour, Susan climbed out and walked to the corner where the life guard was adjusting the harness to lift David out.

"Hi, Mrs. Rowland. We're all through. This will be his last visit for awhile."

"I know," Susan said. Dr. Kernowsky had explained to her that this kind of therapy was reserved for patients who were making progress.

"Thanks for your efforts," she said to the therapist.

She brushed a lock of damp hair out of David's unseeing eyes and walked away.

The Opera House lights reflected off of the river in the falling snow. Paul and Susan stood at the window with drinks in hand.

"You seem quiet tonight," he said.

"I guess it's just a relief to finally make a decision."

"I am sorry, you know." He placed a hand on her arm.

She turned to gaze out at the snow, and his hand fell away.

"Let's go in now," she said.

When the horn concerto began, Susan closed her eyes. She was carried away by the music, free of ordinary existence. Afterward, it took a few minutes for her to realize that Paul was speaking.

"You can take it with you tonight," he was saying.

Later she did take the little white envelope when he handed it to her in his rumpled bed. He placed a hand on her hip and drew her close.

"Be careful," he said.

"I've planned carefully," she said. "No one will know when I enter David's room."

"You know this is medication he takes regularly, so there should be no serious suspicion that anyone meant to harm him."

"I'm sure of that," she said.

"I'd wish you good luck, but that doesn't seem appropriate. I'll just wish that everything goes smoothly."

"I'm sure it will," she said. A sob caught in her throat before she could stop it.

Paul held her in his arms until she gently pushed him away and gathered her clothes.

"I suspect there will be publicity, so you won't need to call me—afterwards," he said.

Susan nodded. "I'm sure you'll find out from the media. At least you will know that my intentions were good."

"The next concert?"

"Let's not talk about it just now," she said. "I need to concentrate on getting through the next few days."

"Of course."

She gave him a rueful smile and then walked out into the snow.

Susan dressed with care, donning soft-soled shoes and black slacks and sweater. She chose pearl earrings to soften her look and a shot of whiskey to strengthen her resolve. David had given her the earrings in Hawaii after a day of snorkeling and kayaking at Kailua. A single tear ran down Susan's face. She brushed it away and finished her whiskey.

The odor of the nursing home hit her the moment she cracked the door open: that repulsive mixture of medicine, food and illness. Susan tried not to breathe deeply and stepped into the building. She bypassed the front desk and walked the long way around the back hall past the nursing station. The nurses were used to her evening visits and wouldn't be able to recall exactly when she had entered the wing.

David was asleep, of course. Even in sleep, his face looked strained, his jaw moving restlessly. She pulled the can of juice from her coat pocket and took the white envelope from her purse. She shook out six tablets onto the top of the can and crushed them with her car keys. Quickly brushing the powder into the juice, she stared into the mirror as she swirled the can.

Moving to the head of the bed, she leaned down and kissed David's pale forehead.

Then she sank into the chair next to him and drank the juice in one long swallow.

Foolproof
By Colin Conway

"Quiet or she'll hear us," Kerry whispered as he prepared to turn the doorknob with his left hand. I noticed that a gun had come from somewhere and appeared in his right hand.

"Sorry," I whispered with a lisp. My tongue had grown thick with fear and excitement. All I wanted to do was run away. Kerry had told me this was going to be a burglary. Now it was apparent that the house was not empty and the gun Kerry brandished told me that his whole story had been a lie.

Kerry had found me two weeks before at the mini-mart where I was clerking. I watched him climb out of an old Mazda 626 and strut across the parking lot.

As he neared the building, he lifted his sunglasses and pushed them back on his head, tucking his long strands of blonde hair behind his ears.

The store's door opened with a chime, and Kerry stepped in. The multi-colored strip hanging next to the door told me Kerry was six-foot-two, several inches taller than me.

Kerry strode toward the beer cooler, his eyes never looking my way. He yanked open the cooler and grabbed a Budweiser tallboy. As he turned and headed toward me he snatched a small bag of Doritos.

He set the items on the counter. "Gimme a hard box of Marlboro reds," he said in his nicotine-scarred voice.

I nodded and reached for the cigarettes.

Kerry dug into his pockets and pulled out a crinkled ten spot. He tossed it on the counter and wiped his mouth.

"Still believe you're straight, amigo?" His voice was low, even though we were the only two in the store.

I nodded as I opened the register.

"So I can't talk you into handing over all that cash?"

I tucked the ten-dollar bill into the appropriate slot and counted out his change. "Cameras," I said without looking toward the electronic eyes. "Besides, it ain't worth violating my parole. I need this job."

Kerry shook his head. "That's the problem with parole, man. The system's always got you by the balls."

"I know," I said, and thought about all of the times Kerry and I had sat in the yard at Walla Walla talking about when we would get outside. We were going to make a name for ourselves.

"You like it?" Kerry asked.

I pushed the register's drawer closed with my hip and handed him his change. "It doesn't have anything to do with like. You want that in a bag?"

"Sure," Kerry said and watched me tuck the beer, chips and smokes into a small brown paper sack.

Kerry took the bag and dropped his sunglasses back over his eyes. He grinned. "I'll be seeing you, Desmond."

"See ya," I said.

Kerry turned and strutted out. The car fired up with a plume of smoke and slowly pulled out of the parking lot.

That night I sat in my studio apartment and re-read an eviction notice. I absently rubbed my St. Dismas medallion as I read.

The Hope Apartments were being renovated for rich fucks and the building's tenants were being tossed onto the street in twenty-seven days.

The building was nothing to brag about. Located in downtown Spokane it housed mostly ex-cons, whores and nut balls. It was a dump and my apartment was a dump inside the dump.

The only thing I had of any value was the St. Dismas medallion, and I carried that with me everyday. My father gave it to me after I was convicted. Dismas, a thief, was hung on a cross next to Christ and is the patron saint of prisoners.

My father had trouble believing I was innocent, but he never stopped loving me as his son. He died while I was in prison.

I continued to rub the medallion, like I did almost every day while in the pen at Walla Walla.

I was trying to stay straight. I didn't want to go back in. Some guys like that life, but for me prison was exactly what the system hopes it will be. It was a hell I never wanted to repeat.

But seeing Kerry walk into the 7-11 looking so happy and carefree bothered me.

I wasn't happy, and I sure as fuck wasn't carefree.

Kerry showed up again at the mini-mart a few days later. He came in with the same walk and the same sunglasses pushed back on his head. He never made eye contact with me as he headed back to the beer cooler and pulled out another tallboy.

When the other customers had left, Kerry walked up to the counter and laid a crinkled twenty on it.

"Interested in doing some work outside of this place?"

"No," I said, and shoved the tallboy into a bag.

As I dug into the register, Kerry leaned in towards me. "Five grand for an hour's worth of work."

"That sounds like a felony, and my freedom's worth more than that."

Kerry smiled. "I'll let you think about it before taking your answer as gospel."

He grabbed the brown paper bag and walked out of the store.

Then that night Kerry showed up at my apartment. I was surprised to see him standing there. He wore a big grin and carried a six-pack of Miller High-Life in his hand.

"Wanna share some of the high life with me?" he asked and lifted the beer to emphasize his joke.

I stepped out of his way and let him into the

apartment.

He walked in and glanced around. "Nice place, Des. How long you been here?"

"Since I got out."

"What's that been? Six months?"

"Seven."

"Seven months. Man, that's awesome. I've been out for almost thirty days now."

Kerry walked over to the little, round kitchen table and its one chair. He set the beers down on the table and saw the eviction notice sitting on it. He slid the paper over with one finger and nodded as he read.

"Where are you staying?" I asked.

"With my baby's momma."

"I thought you said you couldn't trust her."

"I can't. She's a fuckin' whore, but I needed a place to stay and figured why not there." He laughed a little before adding, "I can bang the slut like anyone else, and I don't have to pay no rent."

He had talked about his girlfriend when we were inside. Half the time he was grousing about her, the other times he sounded sad. It surprised me to hear that he'd gone back to her.

Kerry yanked one of the beers free from its plastic cuff and handed it to me. He pulled one loose for himself and popped the top. He raised his beer to me and I tapped mine against his can, not really knowing what good fortune we had to toast.

He slurped from the can and smiled when he swallowed. "Okay, Des, let's talk business."

I sat on the ratty recliner, and it squeaked under my weight. "Man, I ain't doing nothing that will land me back in there."

"Relax, this is easy."

I shook my head at him.

"And foolproof."

I tilted my head. "Nothing is foolproof."

Kerry sipped his beer before continuing with his sales pitch. "Listen, there's this old broad up on the South Hill who is loaded beyond belief. She's widowed, so there's no man around the house. There ain't no dogs, either. Just a bunch of cats. It's ripe for the taking."

"Why are you doing this, Kerry? Do you want to go back?"

Kerry pointed at me. "I ain't afraid of it, if that's what you're asking."

"That's not what I'm asking."

He ran his fingers through his hair. "I'm not going to work for somebody for minimum wage. I'm better than that."

"Fuck you, man."

Kerry smiled. "I'm not saying you're doing something wrong by jockeying a register, but that ain't me."

"Again, fuck you."

"Okay, okay," he said and raised his hands in surrender. "I'm sorry. Listen, I know a guy who knows a guy who wants us to hit this broad."

"Hit?"

Kerry raised his hand to stop me. "I meant rob."

"Why?"

"Because she stole some land from him."

I sipped my beer, thinking about that. Finally, I asked, "How do you steal land?"

Kerry smiled at me. "Through the courts, Des. They do that shit all the time. You know as well as anyone that they're crooked."

"Yeah, I know that, but how do you actually steal land?"

"Do I look like a fucking judge? How the hell

should I know? All I do know is that this guy is willing to give us ten grand to go in there and clean her out. That's five a piece, *mi amigo.*"

"What does he get out of it?"

"Whatever we take, we give to him. And I have a shopping list of places to look and things to take."

I sipped my beer. "How'd this guy find you?"

Kerry shrugged. "Like I said, 'a friend of a friend.' He was looking for someone and my friend got word to me."

"Who's the guy? And who's your friend?"

"Des, you know that's not how this works."

I shook my head and sipped my beer. There was no point in arguing it. Kerry had his own set of crazy rules, and you couldn't get him to break them. He was solid in that way. He would never sell out a friend, but that didn't mean he wouldn't take advantage of one if he could.

"Why did you come to me about this?" I asked.

"You owe me, Des. Remember?"

I remembered. Kerry came to my rescue in the pen when the Aryan Brotherhood braced me. He stood up for me, got them to leave me alone. I would have fought them, but in the end, no one beats the Brotherhood.

"I'll never forget what I owe, man. But I was straight before I went in, and I want to stay straight now."

Kerry ran his finger around the lip of his beer can. "How about revenge? Can I interest you in a little bit of that?"

I leaned forward. "Revenge?"

"Yeah."

"On who?"

Kerry smiled. "Veronica Caldwell."

"Who's Veronica Caldwell?"

Kerry tapped the eviction notice on the table. "She's the bitch evicting your ass."

At first I didn't believe him about the whole Veronica Caldwell thing. He read about it in the newspaper, he said. I showed him that her name wasn't on the eviction notice, but when I pulled out my lease I'll be damned if it didn't turn out that she was listed as the head of the corporation that owned the Hope.

"You see," Kerry said in triumph. "I know what I'm talking about, Des."

Later that night, as I lay on the lumpy mattress that came with the apartment, I wondered about Veronica Campbell. Who was she? What kind of person had that kind of power? What did she think about when she was laying in bed at night? You could bet she wasn't worried about being evicted.

Kerry showed up at the store the next day. The Mazda was still burning oil, but he looked happy as could be when he walked in. He stopped right inside the door and stared at me.

I was ringing up a customer and there were two more waiting in line.

Kerry asked, "Well?" when I glanced his direction.

I nodded yes and he clapped his hands.

"Alright, amigo," he said and left the store.

I finished ringing up the customers, leaned on the back counter and sighed.

It was after 11:30 on Thursday night when we headed up to Veronica Caldwell's house. She lived on Rockwood Boulevard where the houses were huge, and the garages were larger than the apartment I was living in.

I didn't want to do the job at night. She was going to be home, which made no sense, but the guy who was paying us for the job wanted it done at night while she was asleep. He said it needed to go down then, because a burglary while she was in the house would be more dramatic than if she came home to it during the day. The whole thing seems stupid now, but when Kerry was giving me the pitch, it sounded easy and I bought it. He should have been a car salesman.

Kerry spotted her house, but drove past it. It was a massive building, two levels high and so wide it seemed like a couple of houses had been pushed together. We drove another block before Kerry pulled to the side and turned off the engine.

He glanced over at me. "You still okay?"

I rubbed my St. Dismas medal and nodded.

"Good. Let's go." Kerry smiled and climbed out of the car.

The house was alarmed, but Kerry had the security code to the three-car garage. When I asked him how he got the code, Kerry told me that his friend-of-a-friend had done his homework. "This will be the easiest money either of us has ever made."

Kerry tapped in the four-digit code on the security panel outside the garage and the door slid up slowly and very quietly. Leave it the rich to have silent garage door openers.

The garage connected with the house, but the inner door was locked. Kerry pulled out a black pouch of tools and handed me a small flashlight. I held the beam on the doorknob while he set to work on the lock. It took him a few minutes to get it open, but it finally gave.

We stepped inside the house and found ourselves in the kitchen. I quietly closed the door and handed Kerry the flashlight.

He had a map of the house that went along with his laundry list of items to get.

"Let's go and tie her up first."

"What?" I said, trying hard to keep my panicked voice to a whisper.

"We can't afford to have her catch us. This will take a while."

"No," I said. "That wasn't part of the plan."

I turned to go back to the garage and Kerry snatched my arm and turned me back around. "Listen, amigo. You owe me. And if you walk out now, you get nothing. I'm not talking about killing the woman, just tying her up until we're done."

I stared at Kerry until I believed what he said. We weren't going to hurt the woman. We only needed more time to do the job.

"Alright," I said.

We moved slowly and quietly through the house, using the map as a guide to her room. Her bedroom was on the second floor, so we had to take a flight of stairs which fortunately never creaked once.

Kerry stopped abruptly and I bumped into him, almost knocking him over. "Shit," I blurted.

"Quiet or she'll hear us," Kerry whispered as he prepared to turn the doorknob with his left hand. I noticed that a gun had come from somewhere and appeared in his right hand.

"Sorry," I whispered with a lisp. My tongue had grown thick with fear and excitement. All I wanted to do was run away. "What's the gun for?" I asked, afraid I knew the answer.

"It's only to scare her."

I shook my head. Tying her up wasn't part of the plan and neither was the gun.

Kerry held up three fingers for a moment. He dropped them one by one until there were none. He opened the door as I realized we had nothing to tie the woman up with.

Kerry bent over as he moved into the room. I followed him in, hunkered down in the darkness.

Kerry pointed his small flashlight toward the bed.

I breathed a sigh of relief when we found the bed empty. It was neatly made and hadn't been slept in.

Kerry turned toward me with a confused look. He pulled out his map of the house and studied it. "This is her room. Where the hell is she?"

He stood up and shoved the map back into his pocket. "We need to find her," he said.

"Maybe we got lucky and she's out for the night," I whispered.

"We need to find her," he said, his voice filled with panic.

"Why?"

Kerry waved me off and walked into the hallway as I took a final look around the bedroom. A shotgun blast shook the house. Kerry appeared in the doorway briefly, pushed backward by the force of the blast, then crumpled to the floor. He didn't move after hitting the ground.

I crouched down and moved to the wall, hiding behind a big wooden dresser. I struggled to swallow as my throat closed in on itself.

"I know you're in there," an elderly woman's voice said. "I've already called the police."

My heartbeat was in my ears now, and I looked for an escape route. The window was the only option, but we were on the second floor, and I had no idea what was below.

"If you come out here, I'm going to shoot you." There wasn't any fear in her voice, which scared me even more.

"I'll stay put until the cops get here!" I yelled. My voice sounded like it was coming from the bottom of a well. I moved toward the window, hoping to escape.

"Did my son put you up to this?"

I eyeballed the drop to the ground. There were bushes underneath the window, with a small fence protecting them from the rest of the yard.

"*He* sent you boys here, didn't he?"

My hands shook as I unlatched the window and tried to lift it. The damn thing didn't budge. I looked closer at window sill. It had been painted shut.

"Are you working for my son?" she asked.

I spun around, looking for something to pry the window open. There was nothing except a heavy book nearby. I picked it up and was about to throw it through the window when the old woman said, "If you throw that book, I'm going to have to shoot you."

I glanced over my shoulder and saw a woman in her late sixties at the doorway holding a shotgun. I carefully put the book down on the nightstand.

"And I don't really want to shoot you," she said.

"Then let me go."

"That wouldn't be right, would it?"

She cradled the gun as carefully and confidently as a hunter.

She saw me watching the shotgun. "Don't worry, I'm pretty handy with this thing. That's the benefit of having a father who liked hunting. Why don't you sit down," she said, "And we'll wait for the police together."

I sat on the bed,.

"Why did you come here?"

"My friend asked me to."

"You came to kill an old woman because your friend asked you to?"

I shook my head. "We weren't going to kill you. Just rob your house."

"Do you really believe that?"

I nodded.

"Okay, then, why'd you come to this house?"

"Someone came to Kerry," I said with a nod toward the body on the floor. "Kerry made the deal."

"Did you meet that someone?"

I shook my head no.

"Why would you go along with him then?"

"Revenge," I said softly.

"Revenge?" Veronica asked.

"You're evicting me from the Hope."

"Oh, a vendetta," Veronica said. "Tell me, how long is your parole?"

"Huh?"

"There are only two types of people who live in the Hope—ex-convicts and mental patients. You don't look crazy to me."

"Thirty-six months," I said.

"Three years of parole. You must have done something bad. This probably won't go well for you when the police show up."

I could hear sirens in the distance.

"This will be bad for me," I said. I lowered my head and stared at my feet. Tears welled in my eyes as I thought of more years in prison.

"Do you want a way out of this?"

I met her gaze. Images of prison blazed in my mind. "Yes," I said flatly.

I don't know what she told the police because I was gone before they arrived. I walked out of the house trying to look like a man with all the time in the world. I had a long walk home to think about the events of the evening and the agreement I had just made with Veronica Caldwell.

It was late the next Saturday night when I walked up to a large house in the Blackstone development. A house like this cost more money than I'd see in a lifetime, and this neighborhood was lousy with them.

I rang the doorbell, and after a few moments the door opened slightly. Behind it I could see a man in his late forties. He had a round face with small eyes under big reading glasses. The hair on his head was thinning badly.

"Yes?"

"James Caldwell?"

He looked me up and down before answering. "Who's asking?"

"One of the guys you hired to visit your mother."

His eyes narrowed. "What do you want?"

"The money you promised."

"You didn't hold up your end of the bargain, and you made a mess of the whole affair. You're not getting a cent."

I kept my anger in check. "My friend is dead. Either you pay me, or I go tell the cops what I know."

He thought about it for a moment. Finally, he stepped back from the door and let me in.

"My family will be home soon," he said.

"You don't have a family."

"How do you know..." he began.

"Never mind. Get me the money," I said.

"Wait here." He turned.

I grabbed his arm. "I'll go with you."

He hesitated then led me to a back office. I watched him open a closet door to reveal a safe on the floor. "The money's in there," he said.

"Get it."

He unlocked the safe and pulled out an envelope. "This is the ten grand I promised your friend."

I took the envelope and flipped it open. Green bills were stuffed inside.

"Ten grand is a lot for a robbery," I said.

"Robbery? Why would I want you to rob her?"

I tucked the envelope into my back pocket. "Yeah, why would you want that," I said.

He closed the safe and stood up. He brushed his pants before asking, "How'd you know it was me that hired you guys? I thought I was careful."

"You were careful. I wouldn't have known your name or where you lived if your mother hadn't told me."

James' mouth opened slowly, like a dying fish.

Eight years ago, I went to prison for accidentally killing a man.

This time it wouldn't be an accident.

Hired Help
By Steve Oliver

Spokane, 2138 A.D.

Stanley Mulkens had fallen in love with a woman not his wife. It was the oldest of stories and yet the newest for she was not really a woman at all, but a robot built and programmed to look and act like a woman. And the clever Japanese, who had designed her, had been so successful that Stanley had lost his heart and some of his mind and thought about her nearly all the time.

When he wasn't thinking of the robot nurse Kimiko, Stanley, a stolid, middle-aged pharmacist who still considered himself a dangerously sexual beast, thought about killing his wife. He didn't think of it in those terms, however. He didn't think to himself, *I want my wife dead,* or *I'll be glad when my wife is dead.* He thought things like, *Martha has suffered for so long. It's been so hard for her. I hope that her suffering ends soon.* This type of thought had crossed his mind from time to time over the seven years since his wife had become an invalid. But with the arrival of the robot nurse Kimiko, purchased with healthcare dollars to care for the homebound invalid Martha, he thought about ending her suffering daily.

After a few weeks, when Stanley realized that Kimiko was willing to tend to his needs as well, he found his thinking on the subject was changing in ways that were troubling at first, then, as they became more familiar, comforting and reassuring. When he thought of his wife now the phrases that came to mind included his participation. *Perhaps I should help her out of her misery*, he would think, or *She's in such pain—perhaps I can relieve the pain*. The ultimate thrust of the thoughts was unmistakable—the willful killing of his wife.

But Stanley, comforted as he was by Kimiko's companionship and tender sexual attentions, knew that such thoughts were dangerous. He still loved his wife. And he had scruples. But most importantly, he was a pharmacist and the only way he could think to end his wife's suffering gently was with the tools of his trade. As both husband and pharmacist his name would be on the top of any suspect list in big bold letters.

For a time, Stanley considered openly enlisting Kimiko's aid, but soon thought better of it. One of the things that he loved about her was her purity, her set of software-generated absolute values. She was an innocent, even in her sexual relationship with him, for it was based on the Japanese cultural view of sex as a joyful and kind act separate from the strictures of a love bond. She had been programmed to please, to provide comfort and affection, and if not love, a very good imitation of it.

But Stanley would not be able to provide this act of mercy for Martha on his own. He wanted her to die painlessly, peacefully and he did not want to take the blame—either from the police or from Martha—should he fail and she find out. And the police had a substantial advantage. Somewhere, something would be recorded—a house camera, or a mini-robot, or a cleaning droid, or a micro-robot, one of these would tell on him. No, if Martha were to be killed it could only be done with one of the medications already administered by her own nurse—without the nurse or Martha being any the wiser. He would have to go to one of the virus hackers, the underground software vendors who paid for their drugs and sex by infesting the cybernetic universe with criminal agents moving through the digital ether.

These criminal hackers, like all human software engineers, were excluded from legal software work, work now performed in a more effective, orderly and secure way by software agents and their allies among the robots. The remnants and descendents of the human software community, now doomed to lives of sloth and indolence, got their revenge by producing sly little pieces of code, either for their own malicious ends, or on contract for others. These miscreant engineers introduced their evil little programs into the software universe by hacking wireless portals that could not be fully protected.

The police, still mostly human, had too few neurons to put into this fight against the software diseases that came and went unnoticed as transient infections that stole money, destroyed data, and sent false messages of love to strangers in far lands. The viruses were tolerated as part of the price for the wonders of the digital age. While they caused much mischief and loss of property, few of them caused death.

Without thinking about what he was doing, Stanley began spending his lunch hours frequenting the bars on East Sprague, run by broken-down robots and frequented by down-and-out software engineers who had gone from being masters of robots to being their servants and now to merely being superfluous.

Stanley sat uncomfortably in the dim light of the bar. He did not know how to hire a killer. You needed someone who would do a bad deed and, yet somehow be trustworthy and honest. He couldn't ask for resumes. He couldn't post a notice on a bulletin board. So he sat at the bar and drank a clear alcohol that reminded him of the evergreen trees of the nearby mountains and waited for something to happen.

After a few days of this his attention focused on a red-headed man who was in the bar every day and whose skin was nearly translucent. He sat at the corner of the bar near Stanley and nursed the same drink as Stanley, a synthetic alcohol tinged with a pine-based paint thinner.

The red-haired man approached Stanley first, evidently sizing him up as a man out of place in the seedy bar. He picked up his drink and moved a few stools nearer to Stanley. The man studied Stanley with blood-shot blue eyes and said, "What do you want? What are you after?"

"I'm just having a drink," Stanley replied, excited that something was happening and frightened at the same time.

"You don't need a drink. You're looking for something else. It can't be women—the whores on the South Hill are a lot better looking than they are out here. I suppose you could be looking for a local boy."

Stanley frowned in disgust, as if he had been asked to disrobe at a church service.

"I guess it's not a boy," said the man. "So you want something else. You need someone to write a little illegal code. What do you want to do—get into a bank account, change a court ruling?"

"I do need a little, uh, technical help," Stanley managed to say.

"My name's Garth," said the man. "Buy me a drink and tell me what you need." He held out his hand, and Stanley shook it.

Stanley put his credit chip on the counter and told Garth his story.

Garth didn't seem bothered that the software needed was illegal nor that it would cause the death of another person, though Stanley made it clear what he wanted was to put his wife out of her misery. Garth took a few notes with his wrist-mounted digital assistant as he drank six or seven drinks. Stanley was beginning to think Garth was dragging the conversation out to get more liquor, but before much longer Garth said, "I'll do it. It will take a few days, but I can find a way. You'll have to pay my drink tab for the next year. That's all I need."

For the next few days Stanley returned to his routine—going to work in the morning, coming home to sit with Martha for an hour or two before spending the rest of the evening with Kimiko.

The times with both his wife and his lover were poignant. The one would soon be gone forever, and he would miss her. The other would finally be the exclusive love of his life.

As he spent his evenings with Kimiko, he was amazed at how perfect she was. There were very few signs that she was a robot. Her flesh and the soft material beneath mimicked the flesh and blood of a real-life girl except that in some indefinable way it was softer and more lovely to touch. Even the silences that were the result of software updates provided wirelessly by her manufacturer were charming. She assumed the demeanor of a sleepy person who could be cuddled and hugged, and her CPU still had the power to allow her to return small kisses and shift her position as if in response to his hugs. Most of the time, even when she wasn't updating her software, she said nothing. It was what he had always wanted his wife to say.

It was more than a week before Stanley got a message from Garth. It was a simple message left on the flash memory of his phone so that when it was deleted it would be gone forever: "Today's the day." It was their signal that he was to meet Garth.

"Buy me a drink," Garth said upon seeing Stanley. "I have news."

Stanley signaled to the bartender, a sullen robot of Eastern European manufacture who had once been covered in a cheap, flesh imitation similar to Naugahyde, but who now sported skin and cotton stuffing in about equal proportions. The robot's skin reminded Stanley of an old davenport he had once owned.

"What have you found out?" asked Stanley.

"For one thing, she's not a nurse."

"But she takes care of my wife."

"She's not *fundamentally* a nurse—she doesn't understand medical principles. It's not in her firmware. It's an add-on package of software. She doesn't know what might kill a person. She does what her software package says to do without question."

"What does that mean?" Stanley was a software innocent. He knew that software ran everything in the world, but he didn't know how it worked and he was afraid of anyone who did.

Garth smiled. "I can change one number and your wife will peacefully pass away."

Stanley was silent. It was a dream come true. He didn't want to say anything that would jinx the moment or make it untrue.

"Buy me another drink," said Garth. "You owe me one."

Stanley signaled the bartender. He still couldn't bring himself to say anything that might be inappropriate, or spoil the moment, such as, "When can you do it?" He was thinking about how to broach the subject when Garth spoke.

"I already did it," he said, as he downed the final swallow of his drink.

"What?"

Garth looked at his watch. "I changed the number this morning. Your nurse girlfriend just gave the fatal dose. Your wife will be dead by the time you get home."

Stanley would have preferred an opportunity to say goodbye to Martha, a farewell moment with her even though she would not have known it was a farewell. He had loved her for many years despite his dissatisfaction with their life together.

He made the best of the situation, buying Garth another drink before making arrangements for his accomplice's bar tab. He caught an air cab back to his house, making one stop on the way to buy flowers for Kimiko.

The mortuary limousine was at his house when he arrived and he was greeted matter-of-factly by the robot driver, who required that he identify himself and sign numerous forms before the limousine ushered his wife of twenty-five years toward eternity.

After Stanley had stood in the driveway for a few minutes, his throat swollen with emotion, he turned toward the house and his new life, his chest swelling with joy. With new resolve in his step he strode toward the front door.

Inside he found Kimiko waiting for him, but she did not greet him with a kiss as was their custom. She was standing in the foyer next to a large coffin-sized crate that he recognized as the box she had been shipped in.

"Kimiko, what's this?"

She replied in an uncharacteristic machine-like mode usually reserved for communications with her manufacturer. "This is my shipping container," she said flatly. "I am to be returned to the factory."

"But I don't want you to be returned to the factory."

"I must be returned. I am defective. Diagnostics show my nursing function has malfunctioned. I am guilty of manslaughter and will be destroyed to satisfy legal requirements."

"I need you!" said Stanley. "You are not defective."

"Please ship me UPS ground," said Kimiko. "They will not pay for air freight." With that she climbed into the coffin-like box and pulled the lid over her face.

As he heard the sound of relay-operated locks snapping into place Stanley sat in the chair by the front door.

Then, and for the first time since he was a child, Stanley began to cry.

Under Angel's Wings
By Barbara Curtis

Columbia County, 1938

Trying to describe Grandma Billie was like trying to stop a stream of water with your bare hands. One minute you thought you had it and in the next it slipped right away from you. Like many women of her generation, Grandma Billie had suffered a lifetime of small insults and indignities. The final one came here, at her funeral, with the preacher mispronouncing her given name, Wilhelmina, throughout the service.

I squirmed in the hard pew every time he said, "Wilma." Right then and there, I determined that whoever would facilitate me in meeting my Maker would at least be able to introduce me to Him by my correct name. Sweat trickled down my neck, and my dress was soaked clear through where baby Ruthie slept beneath my chin. Beside me, Donnie fanned himself with the stiff funeral card and leaned his head listlessly against my arm.

Carl was home. He hadn't the wherewithal to pull himself into his tie and vest to make a proper appearance with his wife. Grandma Billie and I had that in common. We had both managed to hook up with drinking men.

It was afterwards, at Aunt Elsie's house, that I first heard mention of my legacy. We had returned from the cemetery, and Aunt Addie and Aunt Elsie were setting dishes of corn and potatoes and platters of ham on the makeshift tables in the back yard. I had retreated to the screened-in back porch to avoid the flies and yellow jackets while I gave Ruthie her bottle. Cousin Eldred gave me a snaggle-toothed grin as he heaved his bulk up the back steps.

"Well, Maxine, I guess you'll be wanting to move into town now."

I shifted Ruthie to my other hip before I spoke.

"What are you talking about?"

"With the legacy from Billie, you won't have to live in that chicken coup."

"El, I don't know about any legacy, and the house I'm in suits me just fine." I set my jaw and stared him down. Trust Eldred to get a dig at me about living in a converted bunk house. I had used the last of my egg money to make it presentable with daisy printed fabric for curtains, and there wasn't one speck of dirt in all three rooms. Eldred shrugged and plodded away toward the outbuildings, and the circle of men sure to be sharing a bottle before the meal.

I didn't think any more about El's comment until the next Tuesday when Dorothy Zimmer from the store down the road stopped by to give me a message in an envelope. It was addressed to Mrs. Carl Hanson, which made me kind of nervous. I'd never received a letter addressed formally to "Mrs. Carl Hanson."

"Would you like some coffee?" I asked.

"No, thanks, I have to finish up deliveries and get back to close the store. I've got Hershel watching it." I understood her concern. Hershel Zimmer didn't have the sense God gave a goat.

I took the envelope in my hands and sat down. Donnie, who had been hiding beneath the oilcloth-covered table, crawled into my lap. I slit the envelope with a kitchen knife and out fell a folded letter. In typed letters it said: "Please arrange to visit my law office at your earliest convenience to take possession of property bequeathed to you by Mrs. Wilhelmina Schwab." It was signed Walter Perkins, Esquire, Dayton, Washington.

I was excited but also daunted at the prospect of getting myself to Dayton. It was certainly a puzzle that Grandma Billie had anything to bequeath and that she'd gone to a lawyer to boot.

One week later, I stepped out of Mrs. Zimmer's truck right next to the cannon in front of the courthouse. Mr. Perkins' office was just across the street, on the second floor of a brick building. Mr. Perkins was short, white-haired and spoke with a soothing voice. "I'll just ask you to sign this document stating that you've taken possession of the property."

"Yes, sir." I removed my cotton gloves and signed the paper.

Mr. Perkins opened a large black safe and took out a cloth sack. He pressed it into my hands and walked me to the door.

I knew when I had arranged the ride into Dayton with Dorothy Zimmer that everyone in the county would learn the details of my inheritance before the sun went down, and that's pretty much what happened. Even children Donnie's age could tell you that Maxine Hanson carried home a black velvet box with a big, square-cut emerald ring in it.

The way Carl looked at it made me uneasy, so I waited until he left to do some day work and put the box into a piece of crockery and set it at the back of the root cellar. Carl never did find my hiding place. He never had the time. Someone shot him through the heart with a pistol the day the children and I stayed at Aunt Addie's to help her finish canning eighty quarts of ripe peaches.

The sheriff said it appeared that two men had been at the house. He asked, "Do you know anyone who would have been playing cards and drinking with your husband?"

I said, "Anybody Carl met would have been playing cards and drinking with him."

The family attended our second funeral in a month. This time, Aunt Addie held the dinner afterwards. She served up plenty of peaches.

At home, when the children were tucked into bed, I sat at the table where their father had died to think what to do. At the age of twenty-three, I was a widow with three good dresses, two children and one large emerald ring.

On an impulse, I fetched the velvet box from the root cellar and opened it. The emerald was like something you'd see on a glamour gal in the movies. It didn't seem to bear any relation to Grandma Billie, yet it had been rightfully hers and now it was mine. While I was staring into the box I noticed the tiniest sliver of white at the corner. I meant to brush it away, but when I got my fingers on it, the box lining pulled loose. The white was a paper folded many times. I smoothed it out on the oilcloth and leaned close to read the writing: "Angels will care for you if you look for them."

Suddenly I felt so tired I didn't even have the energy to walk back to the root cellar. I put on my nightgown, slipped that ring under my pillow and fell right to sleep. It must have acted as a talisman, because in the morning I knew just what to do.

I scrubbed Donnie and Ruthie, packed my striped cardboard suitcase, and put on my Sunday hat to take the bus to Spokane. Miss Hazel McLaughlin had been my mother's childhood pal. She had urged me to come for a visit many times, and now I'd take her up on it. We would stay with Miss McLaughlin while I looked for gainful employment.

From the moment we stepped off the bus, I knew this wasn't going to be like farm life. Spokane was a lively and crowded place. It took me several nights before I could sleep through the sounds at Miss McLaughlin's Fourth Avenue Apartment. The city was so sad and so wicked, what with bunches of folks hopping off freight cars and doing most anything to keep body and soul together.

I had the good luck to find work right away as a waitress in the downstairs lunch counter at the Kress Department Store. The cook, Jake Morgan, chewed an unlit cigar and barked questions at me.

"Can you carry heavy dishes?"

"I been carrying as much as any adult on the farm since I was ten years old."

"Are you gonna stay sober and show up for your shift?"

"My late husband did enough drinking for the both of us."

He tossed me a uniform. "Go put this on and start getting lunches out."

I did just that.

It wasn't until I'd taken home my first week's wages that I took notice of the man with the mustache. He sat in my section of the green-tiled counter and always ordered a sandwich: bologna and lettuce, or dried beef and cheese. I paid attention because each day he left me a dime next to his plate. I always hurried to refill his coffee cup.

Then one day he smiled and said, "Maxine, you work too hard. You should lead a life of leisure—eating bon-bons and wearing emeralds."

I tell you I just about dropped the percolator. I kept most of the surprise off my face and answered, "Fat chance of that!"

His words nagged at me, though. When I got back to Miss McLaughlin's place, I slipped the velvet box with the emerald into a stocking and buried it at the bottom of my suitcase. I watched the folks at lunch carefully after that, but nobody seemed to pay me any mind.

'Round about two weeks later I was walking home along Riverside Avenue, admiring the stone lions guarding the bank when a big Packard sedan pulled to the curb. Out jumped the fellow with the mustache. He had another man with him who was built as square as an ice box. Before I could think what to do, they each took hold of an elbow and plunked me into the back seat. I didn't say a word, but I was thinking hard about Ruthie and Donnie—what would happen to them if anything happened to me?

The driver headed the Packard west, downhill towards the river. A gentleman wearing a black topcoat was sitting next to him. I could see white hair beneath his fedora. He said, "You are Maxine Hanson, the granddaughter of Gus and Wilhelmina Schwab?"

I couldn't get my voice to working, so I just nodded.

"I regret that it was necessary for us to meet this way. I'm Vincent Ferrante. I hope we haven't frightened you too badly."

Now that made me mad. As if I wouldn't be frightened at being snatched off the sidewalk and put into an automobile with strangers! I was working up to give him a piece of my mind when he said, "I assure you we mean you no harm. Your grandfather was a business associate of mine."

I said, "That must have been awhile ago. Grandpa Gus died in 1923."

"Yes, indeed. I am well aware of the date of his death. Young lady, you have a ring from your grandmother in your possession. I would like to see it, if you please."

I lifted my chin and said, "You can look at it, but I'm not going to let you take it. It's my rightful inheritance."

He shifted so he could look me straight in the face and smiled. "You are indeed Gus Schwab's relation. I don't wish to take your jewelry, merely to inspect it."

"I guess you can do that," I allowed. He could, in fact, have done whatever he pleased.

We drove to Miss McLaughlin's apartment house, and the mustachioed man went in with me.

"You stay in the hallway," I told him. "No sense in upsetting everyone."

I hurried inside.

"Maxine, I was starting to worry. Supper is on," Miss McLaughlin said.

"I'm sorry. I'll be right back," I called as I pulled my suitcase out from under the day bed and grabbed the velvet box.

Her eyes got big when she noticed my escort at the door. "Is everything—?"

"It's fine. Just give me a few minutes."

We trooped back out to where the Packard waited at the curb. Mr. Ferrante examined the box and found the slip of paper. His eyes twinkled as he said, "Mrs. Hanson, you have been most helpful. My apologies for your inconvenience. You will be compensated for your trouble."

With that he placed the ring in my hands and touched his fingers to the brim of his hat. I stood at the curb with my skirts flapping in the breeze while that sleek sedan disappeared around the corner.

A few days later, a man handed me an envelope as I was clearing away the remains of his blue plate special. "For your trouble," he said.

I put the envelope in my pocket and waited until the crowd cleared out a bit before I peeked inside it. What I saw made me sit right down to catch my breath. That envelope was chock full of bills. When I counted them that night after everyone had gone to sleep, it turned out to be close to five hundred dollars!

I didn't waste any time pondering my good fortune. I bought a house on North Astor Street. Folks back home figured I had found a generous buyer for my emerald ring. Truth to tell, I kept the ring, and a year later, I bought a pair of earrings to go with it. I wore them when I went out for cocktails with Emmitt Roth, the man with the mustache. I wore them again when I met Vincent Ferrante for dinner at his restaurant.

"You look lovely in emeralds, Mrs. Hanson," he told me.

"Thank you. I believe I owe their purchase to your generosity," I told him.

He made a little gesture with his palms up. "I like to reward people who are helpful. You can be thankful that your late grandfather gave you an opportunity to assist me."

He poured us each a glass of wine and we set to eating our spaghetti.

Afterward, Mr. Ferrante had his driver take me home where the children and Miss McLaughlin were already in bed, Miss McLaughlin being my companion and housekeeper now. I got into a dressing gown and used some Pond's face cream before I sat in the front parlor of my house that was bought and paid for with the angels' money.

Miss McLaughlin was the one who had finally spilled the beans about Grandpa Gus. She saw me the night I hid the velvet box in my stocking, so I told her about the man at the lunch counter talking about emeralds.

"Sit down and let's talk," She said. "It seems in 1923 Gus made regular trips up north of Hillyard to meet a fellow who came down from Newport with cases of Canadian whiskey. Now there's no real shame in that. In those days every man with a milk truck, ice truck or coal wagon took bottles somewhere. One woman even delivered hooch by hiding the bottles in a baby buggy and tucking her baby in on top of them. But your Grandpa was working for Vincent Ferrante, and the police were suspicious. One night he figured out he had been followed. According to the man from Newport, Gus warned Ferrante, and turned off the road to hide the money. Sure enough, the cops showed up a short time later, but they couldn't find the money or the whiskey. Their story was that Gus was shot trying to 'flee the authorities.' As a condolence, Mr. Ferrante gave Billie the emerald ring. The Newport man turned up at the funeral. He gave Billie a note Gus had scribbled to her that night, something about angels. It was an odd message, considering neither Gus nor Billie took to religion much."

The day after Miss McLaughlin told me about Grandpa Gus, I caught the bus to Hillyard and hitched a ride up the road on a bakery truck. The driver asked, "Which family are you looking for?"

I answered, "I'm not looking for a family; I'm looking for angels."

He haw-hawed and rubbed his chin. "I know a place just about across the road from the oil refinery where you can see angels."

"Oh?" I leaned forward eagerly.

"It's a ol' graveyard." His haw-haw laugh burst out.

I sat back. It was better than nothing.

"Set me down there, then."

I walked into the trees, to a small clearing. No sign marked it as a cemetery, but there were about a dozen grave markers. In the first row I found the right one. It had a child's name with dates only four years apart. On each side of the stone was a winged angel.

I found a sharp stick. It took awhile to dig, but the metal box wasn't buried very deep. Now I may be a farm girl, but I'm not dumb. I took only about half of the money and rearranged the rest so's to make the box look full. Then I placed the box back in the earth and stomped down the dirt, wiping away any trace of my shoes. I guess when Mr. Ferrante's men got there they were so happy to find the long lost cashbox that they never noticed the dirt was pretty loose.